MISTLETOE

✳ ✳ ✳ ✳ ✳ ✳ ✳

MISTLETOE

✳ ✳ ✳ ✳ ✳ ✳ ✳

FOUR HOLIDAY STORIES BY

Hailey Abbott

Melissa de la Cruz

Aimee Friedman

Nina Malkin

SCHOLASTIC INC.

NEW YORK ✳ TORONTO ✳ LONDON ✳ AUCKLAND ✳ SYDNEY
MEXICO CITY ✳ NEW DELHI ✳ HONG KONG ✳ BUENOS AIRES

No part of this publication may be reproduced, stored in a retrieval system, or transmitted in any form or by any means, electronic, mechanical, photocopying, recording, or otherwise, without written permission of the publisher. For information regarding permission, write to Scholastic Inc., Attention: Permissions Department, 557 Broadway, New York, NY 10012.

ISBN 0-439-86368-6

Compilation copyright © 2006 by Scholastic Inc.

"Have Yourself a Merry Little Breakup" copyright © 2006 by Alloy Entertainment
"The Christmas Choos" copyright © 2006 by Melissa de la Cruz
"Working in a Winter Wonderland" copyright © 2006 by Aimee Friedman
"Scenes from a Cinematic New Year's" copyright © 2006 by Nina Malkin

12 11 10 9 8 7 6 5 4 3 2 1   6 7 8 9 10 11/0

Printed in the U.S.A.
First printing, October 2006

MISTLETOE

✳ ✳ ✳ ✳ ✳ ✳ ✳

CONTENTS

* * * * * * *

WORKING IN
A WINTER
WONDERLAND

By Aimee Friedman

* * * * * * *

"Did you ever notice something?" Maxine Silver said into her cell phone as she strode down Columbus Avenue, passing tinsel-decorated shops blasting holiday hits at full volume. Each time a puffy-vested, bag-laden customer emerged beaming from a store, a snippet of some Christmas song would float out toward Maxine on the crisp December air.

"Santa baby, slip a sable under the tree for me . . ."

"Jingle bell time is a swell time . . ."

"All I want for Christmas is . . ."

"What?" Maxine's best friend, Tara Sullivan, asked on the other end of the line, her mouth full of what Maxine guessed were gingerbread cookies.

"There's a severe shortage of Hanukkah songs," Maxine replied, using her free hand to tug her fringed burgundy scarf higher up her chin. Her teeth chattered as she darted across West 76th Street, a yellow taxicab honking in her wake. She wished she'd remembered to put her knit cloche hat on over her shaggy-short dark hair when leaving her apartment minutes before. Though who could blame her for rushing to escape the embarrassment of her mom and new stepdad, who'd spent the morning frying potato pancakes and inventing pet names for each other? Maxine had been home on winter break for only three days, but she was pretty much ready to go back to college.

"How about, um, the dreidel one?" Tara offered, her voice as sweet as gingerbread itself.

Maxine grinned, picturing Tara standing in the kitchen of her grandparents' house, auburn hair tied back in a ponytail and fair skin flushed with concern. Maxine and Tara had been fused at the hip from the first week of ninth grade on, but since starting their respective freshman years in September — Maxine at Wesleyan, Tara at the University of Chicago — the two girls had only seen each other twice, over Thanksgiving weekend. Tara and her family were spending Christmas in Oregon, so Maxine was all but living for New Year's Eve, when her other half would return to throw a gold-and-white-themed bash at her swank Riverside Drive apartment.

"You know what I mean," Tara added, and, to Maxine's growing amusement, shifted into slightly off-key singing. There was a reason the girl had been the drummer, and not the lead singer, of The Torn Skirts, their short-lived high school band. "Dreidel, dreidel, dreidel, I made it out of —"

"My point exactly, Tar." Maxine giggled, passing a row of fresh green trees stacked up outside a corner grocery. Stray pine needles crunched beneath the soles of her slouchy vintage boots. "Talk about pathetic. Why 'I made it out of clay'? Clay is so . . . low-rent. Why not at least pashmina?" She rolled her big brown eyes.

4

Tara's warm laugh bubbled down the line. "Max, I'm sorry. I know you think Hanukkah always gets the shaft."

Maxine sighed and came to a stop in front of the tiny, trendy boutique Pookie & Sebastian. "Sweetie, I've gotten used to it after eighteen years. It's like when I was in grade school — somehow, I believed in Santa Claus, but I just figured he didn't believe in *me*."

The two girls broke into laughter again but then Maxine bit her lip. For all her teasing, she *did* get a little bummed around Christmastime. How could she not? What with the mammoth tree glimmering in Rockefeller Center, Starbucks hawking their special eggnog lattes nonstop, and ninety percent of her friends celebrating elsewhere, Maxine couldn't help feeling left out of the fun. True, she had once loved Hanukkah — the flickering candles in the menorah, the chocolate coins wrapped in bright foil, the plastic top spinning between her fingers — but that was back when her family had still been seminormal.

"New Year's will lift your spirits," Tara assured her cheerfully. "Pun intended, because my parents are totally stocking the apartment with top-shelf alcohol. And speaking of which, have you made any headway toward getting The Dress?"

"I'm drooling over it as we speak," Maxine replied, gazing in rapture at Pookie & Sebastian's window display. Amid boughs of holly and twinkling fairy lights, a mannequin modeled the impossibly perfect dress that Maxine had spied two days ago, and to which she now made regular pilgrimages. Pale gold and floaty, with spaghetti straps, an empire waist, and a full, gauzy skirt, The Dress was the heavenly union of haute couture and hipster: in other words, Maxine's style exactly.

That first day, she'd bounded inside to try it on, fingers tightly crossed; Maxine was so petite ("pixie-esque," Tara liked to call it, while Maxine preferred the more economical "shrimpy") that she often had to buy children's sizes. But, as she'd excitedly observed in the fitting room mirror, this very grown-up dress fit her just right. Best of all, its color made it ideal for Tara's chichi soiree — to which, Maxine had reminded herself with a flutter of nerves, her best friend was inviting their entire high school class. Including Heath Barton.

Gorgeous, deep-voiced, cooler-than-thou Heath Barton, whom Maxine had spent the better part of high school lusting after. And even though she'd kissed two boys in college, the thought of Heath, whom Maxine had never kissed, let alone really talked to, still sent tingles down her limbs. She hoped that at Tara's party — emboldened by champagne and this sex-kitten dress — she'd finally have the chance to get her flirt on. Then Maxine had glanced at the square tag hanging from the bodice and her stomach had dropped. Were the gods of fashion mocking her? How could a dress so *clearly* designed for her be so out of her price range?

After an entire crazy, fun, stressful semester of buying art history textbooks, late-night pizzas, and six-packs of Mike's

Hard Lemonade for dorm parties, Maxine had gained a new understanding of the term *flat broke*. The fact that it was Hanukkah — that evening would mark the fourth night of the holiday — was no help. Maxine's family followed the "one big present" rather than the "eight big-ish gifts" philosophy. And since Maxine had already received her gift for the season — a boxed set of Bach CDs, which she had promptly stuffed in a remote corner of her closet — it was too late to ask for the dress. Maxine was criminally behind on her own gift-shopping; that afternoon, she was headed to the Columbus Circle holiday market in search of some cheap-but-respectable presents.

"At this point," Maxine mused aloud to Tara, "the only reasonable thing for me to do would be to get a job." She turned away from the window with a mournful sigh and continued southward on Columbus. The grand white facade, dancing fountains, and brilliantly lit tree of Lincoln Center came into view. Maxine's mom and stepdad were both cellists in the New York Philharmonic, and for one insane instant, Maxine wondered if they could snare her a position there as well — not that her talent for playing bass guitar would get her very far. Maxine *was* passionate about music but, to her mother's chagrin, her tastes ran toward indie bands and garage rock. Maxine pictured herself playing her guitar in the subway, all boho and gritty, as passersby dropped change into the open guitar case at her feet. Then she dismissed the idea; definitely too humiliating.

"Well, you *could* just look for another dress," Tara was suggesting. Then she paused at the sound of raised voices in the background. "Oh, crap, Max, I have to go. My grandfather needs help fastening our giant inflatable Santa to the roof."

"I'll e-mail you later," Maxine promised, snapping her Samsung shut and flinging the phone into her houndstooth messenger bag. As she hurried across Columbus Circle toward the red-and-white-striped booths of the holiday market, Tara's parting advice echoed in her head. Maxine knew her sensible friend had a point; she'd probably be able to find a more affordable outfit in the next couple weeks. But a stubbornness — a determination — had bloomed in Maxine at the sight of that gold dress. And, as she wandered the crowded aisles of the market, her eyes flicking over displays of beaded necklaces, velour gloves, and fat, scented candles, she wondered if a winter-break job might be the only solution. After all, she reasoned, her home life was driving her nuts, and her social life would be laughable until New Year's. If only she had the slightest idea where to find work. She cast a glance at a nearby stall selling hideous winter hats, as if a HELP WANTED sign might be hanging there.

A sudden, near-arctic wind tore through the market, rattling a display of glass bowls. "Damn, it's *cold!*" someone cried in a Southern accent — a tourist, Maxine guessed, who'd been under the mistaken impression that New York City would be balmy on December 17. Shivering, Maxine hurried over to the hat stand, once again cursing herself for leaving her cloche somewhere in her messy bedroom. *Whatever*, she decided as she selected a fuzzy leopard-print number with earflaps. *I'd rather look like a first-class freak than die of hypothermia.* She was adjusting the hat on her head when she heard a familiar male voice behind her.

"Madeline? Madeline Silverman?"

Oh, God. Can it be —

Turning very slowly, her stomach tightening in disbelief, Maxine found herself staring into the almond-shaped, bright hazel eyes of Heath Barton.

Yes, Heath Barton. Here he was, standing smack in the middle of the holiday market. His glossy jet-black hair blew across his dark eyebrows and a smile played on his full lips. Maxine noticed that his leather jacket hung open, revealing a black turtleneck and black jeans ripped at the knees. Dazedly, she wondered why he wasn't freezing, until she realized that his own out-of-this-world hotness must have been keeping him nice and toasty. Maxine felt *her* body temperature climbing by the second.

"Madeline," Heath repeated with utter assurance, his square-jawed face now breaking into a wide grin. "From high school. You remember me, right?"

You could say that.

"Oh . . . sure," Maxine said, doing her best imitation of breeziness. She cocked her head to one side, studying him.

9

"Heath . . . Barton, is it?" As he nodded, eyes glinting, she added, "And it's not Madeline, by the way. I'm Maxine. Maxine Silver."

Not that she necessarily expected Heath Barton to remember her name. Back in high school, he'd been the ringleader of the rich-boy slackers and always had some pouty groupie — Maxine had nicknamed them "Heathies" — on his arm. Ensconced in her artsy circle of friends, Maxine had outwardly mocked Heath and his ilk but, as Tara well knew, went all jelly-kneed at the sight of him. And there'd been certain moments — right after she'd won first prize in the senior year talent contest for her guitar performance of a Clap Your Hands Say Yeah song, for instance — that Maxine had caught Heath shooting her inquisitive glances that had clearly meant *Hmm . . . maybe sometime*. Maxine had been counting on New Year's, but maybe the time was, well, right now.

Or could have been now, had she not been wearing a leopard-print hat with earflaps.

Just as Maxine's hands were reaching up to remove the unfortunate accessory, Heath stepped forward, eliminating the space between them. "Maxine — that's right," he said, laughing softly. "My bad. I was close though, huh?"

He was certainly getting close. Maxine barely had time to notice that Heath smelled like wood smoke and cider and spice — and that he'd somehow become even hotter since high school — before he plucked the ridiculous hat off her head, his fingers brushing her sideswept bangs. As he set the hat down on the counter behind them, Maxine frantically tried to mash her post-hat hair back into some semblance of place.

"Don't do that." Heath chuckled, turning back to her. "You're ruining the cuteness effect."

Oh, damn. Maxine wasn't a big blusher, but now she felt an unavoidable warmth stealing up her neck. "I'll keep that in mind," she replied, grinning back at Heath even as her heart drummed like mad. *Tara, wait until you get my e-mail now!*

"So catch me up, Maxine Silver," Heath drawled, resting one elbow on the counter as his eyes held hers. "College adventures, crimes, scandals, holiday plans?"

Maxine shrugged, not wanting to spoil the enchanted moment with either generic college stories *or* her litany of winter-break woes. "You know, the usual, I guess," she replied, hoping the conversation would steer its way back to the subject of her supposed cuteness.

"I'm *stoked* to be out of New Haven," Heath confessed with a world-weary sigh, running a hand through his floppy hair. "There's nothing like winter in the city — chilling with my boys, helping out my dad at his store —" Heath paused meaningfully, and raised an eyebrow at Maxine. "Oh — I'm not sure if you know who my dad — I mean —" He ducked his head.

Maxine nodded. "I know," she whispered. *Everyone* knew who Heath's father was: Cecil Barton III, owner of Barton's, the sumptuous jewel box of a department store on Fifth Avenue. Maxine remembered the buzz Mr. Barton, in his bow tie and bowler hat, had created at their graduation alongside Heath's mother, who was an equally famous — and stunning — Japanese former supermodel. Naturally, because of his parentage, Heath wasn't only a celebrity in the high school hallways. According to the *New York Post*'s Page Six, he had jammed with Sean Lennon's band, gone skinny-dipping with Nicole Richie, and broken Rachel Bilson's heart. Maxine wondered what a guy like Heath Barton could possibly be doing here, now.

"I'm actually here for my dad today," Heath was saying, as if he'd read her mind. "Doing market research — to check out the competition and all." He straightened up and, with a slight air of distaste, gestured to the packed stalls around them. "Technically I'm supposed to be on my lunch break but we're so swamped at the store that I've got to mix business with pleasure." Maxine was forcing herself not to fixate on the word *pleasure* coming out of Heath's mouth when he rolled his long-lashed eyes and went on. "It's madness over there — one of the salesgirls quit this morning so the manager wasn't giving me a moment's rest. I was all like, 'Mr. Perry, can I at least get a ciggie break?' and he was like —"

"Wait." The word had escaped Maxine's lips almost without her realizing it. *Swamped at the store. Salesgirl quit.* She felt inspiration flooding through her body, making her skin prickle and her breath catch. She found she couldn't move.

"There's — there's an opening at Barton's?" she asked. Furiously, her mind fought to process this incredible piece of information. An opening, just when she most needed a job? An opening at the very place where *Heath Barton himself was working*?

It was a freaking Hanukkah miracle.

"Uh-huh," Heath said distractedly, reaching into his jacket pocket and pulling out a sleek BlackBerry. Then he lifted his head and met Maxine's gaze, which she knew must have been wild-eyed and borderline manic. She tried to compose her features into a mask of glamorous sophistication, but then Heath's own eyes widened, and his lips slowly parted. "Maxine, are *you* interested?" he murmured, and then he tilted his head to one side, clearly sizing her up — though for what, Maxine wasn't sure. Then Heath spoke again, sending all the blood rushing to her face.

"You'd be perfect," was what Heath Barton said. "Perfect for the position."

The flattery roared in Maxine's ears, half-drowning out the rest of what Heath was saying — something about how she should go see Mr. Perry now if she was seriously interested, because those types of positions were usually snatched up right away.

"I can totally stop by Barton's now," Maxine exclaimed, suddenly grateful that her schedule was so empty. She almost burst into laughter over her unexpectedly sweet fortune. "Want to walk back with me?" she added casually, as if the thought of an afternoon stroll with Heath wasn't making her belly flip over.

"I'd love to, Maxine," Heath replied, knitting his brows together, while Maxine decided that she could never tire of hearing her name in his deep voice. "Only I still need to run a couple of errands for my dad. But hey —" He took another step closer, rested a hand on the sleeve of her corduroy jacket, and gave her arm a small squeeze. "Do good, okay? If you get the position, maybe I'll see you at the store tomorrow?"

Forget *maybe*. Maxine Silver was going for the gold.

She could still feel the warmth of Heath's hand on her arm seconds later, as she flew down Central Park South, passing the glitzy entrances to The Essex House and The Plaza, unable to stop grinning. A shopgirl at Barton's! Visions of free Lola lip glosses, marked-down Rock & Republic jeans, and, most tantalizing of all, daily doses of Heath Barton, danced in her head. Maybe the position called for her to fold cashmere shrugs, and Heath thought she'd look "perfect" amidst all that luxuriousness. Maybe while she was folding the goodies tomorrow morning, Heath would swing by and suggest they mix business and pleasure *together*. Maxine giggled out loud at the thought, prompting a curious glance from an all-blond family waiting in line for a horse-and-carriage ride. Normally Maxine would have ignored them, but she was so suffused with goodwill that she waved a mittened hand at the pigtailed little girl.

Her scarf streaming behind her like a victory flag, Maxine

rounded onto Fifth Avenue, where a giant, sparkling white snowflake hung suspended overhead, as it did every holiday season. Panting and a little sweaty from her impromptu work-out, Maxine paused on the corner of 58th Street and stared up at the snowflake as if it were her personal good-luck pendant. *Please, please let me get the job*, she prayed silently. Then, realizing she hadn't primped with an interview in mind that morning, she pulled her compact out of her bag and did a scan of her flushed face, relieved that she'd at least worn her dangly shell earrings. Her hands unsteady, she brushed the powder puff over her upturned nose and across her flushed cheeks, and made one last attempt at flattening her unruly hair. Then, with a swipe of DuWop Hyacinth gloss over her lips, she was as ready as she'd ever be. *You are elegant*, she told herself, imagining the pep talk Tara would have given her had she been there. Tossing her head back, Maxine whirled around and pulled open the heavy double doors of Barton's.

Ah.

Classical music filtered down past the soft white globes dangling from the arched ceiling. The walls were painted a creamy color, except for the farthest one, which was brightened by a black-and-pink mural depicting a high-heeled woman walking a poodle in London. That black-and-pink poodle, Maxine knew, was Barton's logo — the image that appeared on every shopping bag, gift box, and advertisement. It was a little bizarre to associate that frilly poodle with the very masculine Heath Barton, and Maxine pressed her lips together to keep from snorting. *Elegant*, she reminded herself, drifting inside.

Maxine hadn't been to Barton's in years, and now she breathed in everything anew. A long glass perfume counter, dotted with crimson poinsettias in vases, rippled through the center of the store like a clear river. Behind the counter, salesgirls in cowl-neck sweaters and short skirts murmured to one another as they sprayed customers' slender wrists with designer scents. *I could work there*, Maxine realized, meeting one of the perfume girls' artfully smudged eyes. But then there was also the makeup counter across the store, where white-jacketed women and men wielded gold-plated eyebrow pencils. Maxine figured she could be a quick study when it came to doing makeovers.

And then, toward the back of the store, the luckiest of shopgirls flitted through endless racks of clothes like fairies in a colorful forest. Sighing with appreciation, Maxine let her fingers dance over puff-sleeved velvet jackets, silky wrap dresses, and fuzzy, pearl-trimmed cardigans. As she advanced toward the back office, where Heath had told her to go, she passed two winding staircases, and noticed that one led down to a cavernous space devoted solely to shoes. *And* that's *where I want to be stationed*, Maxine decided with a smile, reaching the slightly ajar door to the manager's office.

Maxine knocked once, and then pushed the door all the

way open to reveal a skinny young man with a goatee, wearing a button-down shirt, tie, and burgundy-framed rectangular glasses. He was sitting at a cluttered desk, frantically typing something on a laptop in between taking bites of a Krispy Kreme doughnut. A jar full of candy canes sat on the window-sill, the only nod to the season. This image didn't quite jibe with Barton's high fashion vibe, but Maxine didn't care — she'd made it to the inner sanctum.

"Mr. Perry?" Maxine ventured softly, and the man glanced up from his laptop, lifting his glasses up to his forehead and squinting at Maxine.

"You're lost, honey?" he asked. "The fitting rooms are downstairs, with the shoes —"

"Mr. Perry, Heath Barton told me to come see you," Maxine interjected hurriedly. She felt a small glow of pride at being able to toss that powerful name around.

But to Maxine's surprise, Mr. Perry only sighed and rubbed at his eyes. "Did he? Enlighten me. What could the ever-helpful young heir have sent you here for?" Then Mr. Perry slapped a hand to his cheek and feigned a look of horror. "But *shhh.* We can't be caught talking like that about *the boss's son.*" As he spoke, Mr. Perry pointed over his shoulder to a framed painting on the wall of Cecil Barton III himself, who gazed down imperiously in his ever-present bow tie and bowler hat. "I think the old man's bugged the office, to tell you the truth."

Despite herself, Maxine felt her lips twitch. Mr. Perry seemed like a basket case, but at least he was kind of entertaining.

"Well," Maxine began, casting a look at the paperwork on Mr. Perry's desk and realizing with a sinking sensation that she should have brought her resume. And references. And — oh, God — how could she have been so *stupid*, dashing over here on a whim? Suddenly Maxine understood how glaringly unprepared she was for this job. Besides an obsession with eBay and window-shopping, she had no direct experience in retail. She was filled with the urge to turn around and walk out as surely as she'd come in. They'd never take her at Barton's.

"Yeah?" Mr. Perry prompted, still squinting at Maxine as if she were an oversize insect who'd fluttered her way into his office.

Figuring she had nothing to lose, Maxine took a deep breath and plunged ahead. "Heath told me that there was an opening for a salesperson, and that he thought I'd be —"

Mr. Perry's jaw dropped and he shifted his glasses back into place, now staring at Maxine with unabashed interest. "Perfect," he finished for her, and Maxine felt a chill race down her spine. *The exact same word Heath had used.* "God, yes," Mr. Perry went on, his face lighting up with wonder. "Maybe that kid *hasn't* smoked away all his brain cells. Come in, come in — what's your name?" Mr. Perry asked, motioning for Maxine to take a seat in the chair across from him.

In a matter of minutes, to Maxine's amazement, everything was squared away: Mr. Perry, all excitement, informed her of the pay (which was higher than Maxine had expected) and told her that the position was a temporary one, only running until December 24. Maxine took this as good news, since she'd be returning to Wesleyan in mid-January, and mainly needed the money for the holidays anyway. After she had eagerly agreed to Mr. Perry's request that she start tomorrow at nine A.M. sharp, the manager ceremoniously handed her a few forms to fill out, and that was that.

"You just need to try on your costume, and then we'll be set," Mr. Perry said, getting to his feet and heading toward the wardrobe in the corner. "I'm sure it will fit fine, but it might need to be taken in here and there."

Maxine, who had been hastily signing her name on a dotted line, glanced up, startled. *Costume?* Mr. Perry must have been referring to the white-jacketed uniform Maxine had seen on the makeup people. She was about to ask him if she could get a lesson in applying foundation when Mr. Perry turned toward her with a dramatic "*Voilà!*"

But Mr. Perry wasn't holding up a starched white jacket. No.

He was holding up a bright-green long-sleeved leotard, a red cotton drawstring mini-skirt, green-and-white-striped tights, and a plastic headband with enormous, pointy, green plastic ears on either end.

It was an elf costume.

Maxine's stomach lurched. "Um — I — I think —" *I think there's been a mistake*, she wanted to say, but she was too stunned to force the words from her throat.

"You can change in there," Mr. Perry told her, and gestured to a small adjoining locker room, oblivious to the color rapidly draining from Maxine's face. "It's the employee dressing room."

"But —" Maxine's voice came out raspy, and she coughed. "Where am I supposed to *wear* that?" she whispered hoarsely. Maybe trying on the costume was part of some weird Barton's initiation ceremony. She cast a glance up at Cecil Barton III, who glared back at her.

Mr. Perry furrowed his brow. "Upstairs, doll. In our Christmas Corner? Didn't Heath tell you? Our second floor is devoted to all things Christmas this time of year. That's why, when our only elf quit on us, we needed a replacement so badly."

Maxine felt the pen slip out from between her fingers. It fell to the floor with a clatter.

You have got to be kidding me.

Maxine glanced down at her own signature, her body slowly going numb. Getting to her feet and running from the office seemed like the best possible plan, but Maxine also knew that would be the cowardly way out. Heath had gone to the trouble of telling her about this position, Mr. Perry seemed so hopeful to have her on board, *and* she'd already signed all the forms. . . . The least she could do was try on the stupid costume. The get-up probably wouldn't even fit, or it would look so howlingly awful on her that Mr. Perry would assign her to some other post in the store.

Feeling as if she were moving through molasses, Maxine walked over to Mr. Perry to accept the clothes. Clutching the slippery material, Maxine started toward the dressing room, when, as if from a great distance, she heard the manager speak again.

"We can't forget the shoes, honey," he said, holding out a pair of green satin slip-ons with toes that curled up at the tips. "Without them, the outfit doesn't really work, you know?"

Inside the cramped changing room, as she stripped off her stovepipe jeans and angora hoodie, Maxine had a flashback to the fitting room at Pookie & Sebastian. Only now she wasn't wriggling into a luscious gold dress, but a pair of thick tights and a stretchy, itchy leotard. *Kill me.* She was careful not to face the mirror, even when she adjusted the faux ears over her own, securing them in place with the plastic headband that went over her hair. Next came the shoes, into which Maxine's size-five feet slid with surprising ease. Right as she was bracing herself to turn and survey the damage, Mr. Perry knocked.

"Ready?" he asked and, without waiting for her response, opened the door. "Oh, my," he gasped, his eyes growing round behind his glasses. He clapped his hands together and shook his head from side to side. "Look at *you*."

Cringing, Maxine turned to face her reflection — and her heart sank. Because, in that instant, she understood why everyone had thought her so "perfect" for the job. She *looked* like a goddamn elf, the pointy ears emphasizing her delicate features and close-cropped dark hair, the striped tights and upturned shoes somehow working on her tiny, slender frame. As much as it pained Maxine to admit it, the entire costume — like the dress that had led her here in the first place — fit as if it had been made specifically for her.

And, glancing at Mr. Perry's rapt expression, Maxine knew there was no way she could turn and run out of his office now. She was in too deep. Besides, she reminded herself, she *did* need a job. Any job. And maybe she wouldn't have to wear the elf costume *constantly*. Maybe she could change out of it for her lunch breaks, and hide from Heath the rest of the time.

Facing her new boss, Maxine held her breath and gave Mr. Perry a quick nod.

Yes, sir, I'd love to be subjected to public humiliation.

Mr. Perry smiled and extended a hand toward her, message clearly received. "Welcome to Barton's," he said. "And Merry Christmas!"

"Happy Hanukkah!" Maxine heard her stepdad, Scott Levy, call as she dragged herself into her apartment that evening.

The strains of her mother's cello drifted toward her, along with the rich scent of potato pancakes. Maxine's stomach growled; after the insane events of that afternoon, she was mentally and physically drained.

"Happy happy," Maxine muttered in response, kicking off her boots in the foyer. Her mind still on elves, Mr. Perry, and Heath Barton, she headed into the cozy living room, where her mother sat on a low stool, her curly black hair falling into her eyes as she practiced. Scott's own cello was propped up in the corner, beside the oak bookshelves, but Scott himself stood at the dining room table, holding a box of Hanukkah candles in one hand. The family's glass menorah was perched before him with four candles in place, waiting to be lit.

"Why so glum, Max?" Scott inquired, shooting Maxine a boyish grin. It wasn't all that difficult for Maxine's stepdad to look boyish — because he was only twenty-nine years old. As in: eleven years older than Maxine, and many more years younger than Maxine's mother.

In other words: *ew*.

"They're like the Demi and Ashton of the classical music world," Tara had whispered to Maxine two years before, at the wedding, in a failed attempt to make her feel better.

"Yeah," Maxine had whispered back, fiddling with her wilted bridesmaid bouquet. "Only Scott isn't hot — thank God."

"I got a job today," Maxine replied over the cello music,

reaching for the plate of honey-colored potato pancakes on the table. "At a department store." For obvious reasons, she didn't feel like elaborating. She could just imagine Scott doing some lame Will Ferrell–in-*Elf* impersonation. Studying the menorah and the potato pancakes before her, Maxine couldn't quite believe that in a matter of hours she'd be dressed as one of Santa's little helpers and selling Christmas tree ornaments. Culture shock much?

"Mazel tov, Max — that's so cool!" Scott exclaimed, his expression bright and earnest. As always, Maxine felt a pinch of guilt for how she treated Scott — he wasn't a bad guy, but she wished he'd stop trying so hard to be her BFF. At the same time, she didn't want him playing the Dad role, either. Maxine already had a father — who, at the moment, just happened to be living on a kibbutz in Israel. That was where he'd run off to three years ago, when he'd decided that being an attorney was destroying his hippie soul.

"What's this about a job?" Maxine's mother called. She stopped playing and hurried over to the table, the bell sleeves of her floaty black dress swinging back and forth. Rather than wait for Maxine's response, she snuggled up to Scott, sliding her arms around his neck and running her fingers through his light-brown hair. "I missed you, Shmoopy," she whispered.

I'm going to be ill, Maxine thought, dropping her half-eaten potato pancake on a napkin. "You missed him from all the way across the room?" she couldn't help but ask, rolling her eyes.

"Maxine, please drop the sarcasm for one night," her mother snapped, giving Maxine a quick, dismissive glance before turning her attention back to Shmoopy.

Maxine managed to keep the rest of her comments to herself as Scott lit the menorah and recited the Hebrew blessing. Although it was her second Hanukkah with Scott there, Maxine didn't think she'd *ever* get used to seeing him in the role that had once been her father's. As the small, teardrop-shaped flames wavered on the candles and Maxine halfheartedly joined in singing "Rock of Ages," her throat tightened. Not just because she was feeling nostalgic for Hanukkahs past, but because, watching her mom and Scott hold hands, she felt a pang of longing. Suddenly Maxine wished she were spending this sweet, warm holiday not with her mom and stepdad — or even her real dad — but with someone sweet and warm, an adorable guy who would actually care about the job she'd gotten that day, and want to hold her hand while singing.

Heath. Glancing down, Maxine smiled to herself as anticipation rippled through her. Despite her ten thousand qualms about working in the Christmas Corner, the plain fact remained: She'd be seeing Heath Barton tomorrow — and every single day for the next week. And that, Maxine hoped, might just be worth the epic mortification of those pointy ears.

At nine-twenty the next morning, Maxine, in all her elfin glory, anxiously ascended the winding staircase to Barton's Christmas

Corner. She was about to meet her direct supervisor, Sandy Teasdale, whom Mr. Perry had explained would be waiting for Maxine upstairs. When Maxine had come to his office at nine to pick up her costume, the manager had told her that though she needed to be there early for her first day, the other salespeople didn't show up until around nine-thirty because the store opened to the public at ten. Placing one curly-toed foot on the second-floor landing, Maxine wondered when Heath got in, and her heart leaped.

"Elf?"a brusque female voice demanded, and Maxine gave a start, glancing up.

In the middle of a red-and-green-painted, glitter-strewn space crammed to the hilt with fur-trimmed Christmas stockings, crystal reindeer figurines, life-size silver candy canes, and countless other sparkly objects, stood a tall, unsmiling woman in her mid-forties. She wore a high-necked green tweed suit and green pumps, and her wavy red hair tumbled out from beneath a velvet Santa hat. She was holding a clipboard and scowling at Maxine.

"Sandy?" Maxine guessed, bypassing a tree dripping with ornaments as she crossed the plush red carpet and came to a halt in front of the woman.

Sandy didn't look up from her clipboard as she fired off a stern monologue. "As a Christmas Corner employee, you are responsible for assisting our customers in their quest for the perfect Christmas-oriented item, be it a handmade Advent calendar, a ruby Rudolf nose, or a blown-glass angel. Apart from a half-hour lunch break, you must constantly be on hand to offer purchasing advice, wrap gifts, and spread holiday cheer. Do I make myself clear?"

Maxine gulped. "Um, could you clarify the 'holiday cheer' part?" she asked. She didn't add that she was the least likely candidate to spread anything of the sort.

Sandy nodded briskly. "Once a day, whenever I give the signal, you and the other Christmas Corner employees will gather over there" — she pointed toward a spot near a display of Swiss chocolate snowmen — "and break into a song of my choosing." Sandy cleared her throat and consulted the clipboard. "Today's is 'Winter Wonderland.'"

Maxine wondered if she was being punished for a crime committed in a former life. "The other employees?" she repeated, since it was easier to focus on that development than the song issue. Until now, Maxine hadn't given much thought to the possibility of costumed coworkers who would share in her misery.

Sandy lifted her chin and pointed over Maxine's shoulder. "Here they come now."

Turning around, Maxine watched with mingled trepidation and curiosity as two guys and a girl trooped over. The girl had smooth dark skin, a long swan's neck, and a straight, graceful carriage. She wore her curly dark hair pinned up in a bun, upon which rested a silver tiara. With a stab of jealousy,

Maxine took in the rest of her costume: a strapless white top with gold-dusted wings attached to the back, and a pale pink tutu. Maxine fumed, wishing *she'd* been lucky enough to earn the flattering ballet number. Then she turned her attention to the guys. One of them, who had straight blond hair and looked to be about nineteen, wore a scarlet military-style suit complete with epaulets, gold buttons, and long trousers, and a black box-shaped hat was tucked under his arm. At his side was a short guy of approximately the same age, with tousled, shoulder-length brown hair, who wore a red velour jogging suit. A hat identical to Sandy's swung casually from his hand. Maxine thought she'd never seen an odder band of people.

"Meet the Sugarplum Fairy, the Nutcracker Prince, and Santa Claus," Sandy told Maxine in her flat, hard monotone. Pursing her lips at Santa Claus, she added, "Where on earth is your beard?"

Santa's mouth dropped open and his dreamy eyes widened. "Oh, dude. I knew I forgot *something.*" Scratching his head, he turned and headed back downstairs as Maxine watched him, fighting the urge to crack up.

"Nutcracker, please fill Elf in on the rest," Sandy was saying, now moving toward the cash register at the far end of the floor. "I need to set up the register before we open."

Feeling new-girl-at-school-ish, Maxine turned to face her two colleagues, and raised her eyebrows at them, twisting her hands behind her back.

Nutcracker grinned, his blue-gray eyes dancing. "The first thing I should tell you is that, believe it or not, we all have real names. This is Claudette Lambert," he explained, gesturing to the Fairy, who, to Maxine's surprise, gave her a welcoming smile. "Santa's actually Daniel Matheson, and I'm Avery Prince."

"Prince?" Maxine felt a wry smile tug on her lips for the first time that morning. "For real? So you just swapped 'Avery' for 'Nutcracker' to get this job?" Maxine hoped she wasn't offending the guy; her mom often chided her about being too mouthy.

But Nutcracker — or, rather — Avery, only shook his head, still smiling. "One of those lucky coincidences, I guess," he replied cheerily.

Oh, God. Maxine groaned inwardly. Mr. Blond Sunshine was clearly lacking in the humor department.

When Santa/Daniel returned, hat cockeyed on his head and frothy white beard covering his chin, Maxine hurriedly introduced herself to the trio, accepting the fact that, like it or not, she was one of them now. Then Avery gave her another aw-shucks smile. "Let me show you our wrapping station," he said, his voice brimming with enthusiasm. As Maxine reluctantly turned to follow him, her curly-toed slipper made unfortunate contact with a stack of faux yule logs, and she tripped, stumbling forward a few paces. *Great.* Not like Claudette's prima-ballerina presence wasn't already making her feel like the biggest klutz alive. At least Heath wasn't around to witness her smooth moves.

"Easy there, Ms. Elf," Daniel said, stepping forward and taking hold of Maxine's shoulder. "You cool?" Maxine couldn't make out Daniel's mouth behind the beard but his brown eyes were smiling, and she smiled back. She suspected that Slacker Santa's chill vibe might make her time at the Christmas Corner slightly more bearable.

"I'm grand," Maxine replied with a shrug. "I mean, who doesn't enjoy strolling in elf shoes?" Daniel and Claudette glanced at each other, chuckling.

"Well, our last elf, for one," Avery chimed in with predictable earnestness. He motioned for Maxine to join him at a long counter that was strewn with tubes of red, gold, and green wrapping paper.

"Yeah, why *did* she quit?" Maxine asked, feeling a prickle of intrigue as she walked carefully over to Avery. "Or was it death by embarrassment?"

Avery shook his head. "She got a job at the fry station at Burger Heaven on 53rd Street."

Maxine nodded, her worst fears confirmed. So dunking your gloved hands into vats of hot oil was preferable to working the elf gig at Barton's.

"Anyway, wrapping gifts, in my humble opinion, is the second best part of our job," Avery was saying, resting his boxy hat on the counter and gesturing to the brightly colored tubes. "People are so grateful, when all you've really done is slap on some paper and Scotch tape —"

"Uh, hang on," Maxine cut in, annoyed beyond belief by Avery's ode to gift wrapping. "There's a *first* best part to our job? Like what, leaving for the day?"

Avery glanced at Maxine, furrowing his brow. "Wow. Are you always this cynical?" he asked, his tone matter-of-fact.

Maxine rolled her eyes. She was a native New Yorker, for God's sake — she was allowed a little cynicism now and then. Meanwhile, she'd bet anything that Nutcracker Prince was from the Midwest. He'd probably grown up in a perfect split-level ranch house, called his dad "Pop," and got really, *really* into Christmas.

"My favorite part is the kids," Avery was saying, fastening his stiff gold-trimmed black hat on over his blond head. "You'll see — they get so psyched about the smallest things and —"

"I can imagine," Maxine muttered, picturing a screaming brood of five-year-olds fighting over the display of gourmet candy apples. On cue, she heard a cacophony of excited voices streaming up the staircase, along with a boy whining, "Mom, can I get a toy sleigh this year, please, can I, can I?" Glancing at the bough-of-holly clock above the cash register, Maxine's stomach sank. It was ten o'clock. Barton's was open for business. No turning back now.

"Well, here we go," Avery said, tipping the brim of his soldier's hat to Maxine and flashing her a grin. "Good luck, Maxine."

As Avery marched off, Maxine instinctively scanned the faces of the people swarming upstairs, hoping to catch sight of her crush's messy black hair and sly smile. But Heath was nowhere to be seen, and soon the entire space was so flooded with loud, aggressive customers that Maxine had no time to dwell on finding him.

Haggard-looking nannies with grabby toddlers and snooty uptown moms in camel-hair ponchos all descended upon Maxine at once. *Where are the hand-painted Belgian eggnog ladles? Is that Christmas tree for sale? Do you carry fox-fur stockings or do I need to go to Saks for that?* "Um, it's my first day," Maxine replied, breaking out in a sweat and searching for some colleague to come to her aid. But Sandy was at the register, Claudette was pirouetting around the snow globe display, Daniel was half-dozing behind the gift wrap counter, and Avery was good-naturedly posing for a photo with a pack of hyperactive little boys. Maxine tried to answer the storm of questions as they came, but she was distracted by countless elbows in her ribs and a random baby yanking on her elf ears each time he passed by in his father's arms. The fact that she made it through the morning without getting trampled seemed a small triumph.

Lunch, Maxine learned, consisted of egg salad sandwiches

provided by Sandy, and Maxine wolfed hers down while sitting alone on a carton in the back storage room. So much for changing out of her elf costume and meeting Heath; the half hour barely allowed her time to finish chewing her food and tug up her striped tights, which were bunching around the knees.

By three o'clock, the mad rush had trickled down enough for Maxine to do a quick spin around the Corner, mentally taking note of where the Belgian eggnog ladles and various other items were kept. When an elderly woman cradling a chihuahua demanded that Maxine find her the priciest tree ornament in the shop, Maxine produced a Swarovski-crystal-encrusted star in five seconds flat, and couldn't help feeling a flush of pride. But just as Maxine was handing over the ornament, she heard Sandy calling her and the others over to the chocolate snowmen display.

The singing portion of the afternoon, Maxine realized. Dread gripped her as she watched Sandy set up an iPod and Bose speakers while Daniel, Avery, and Claudette gathered in a semicircle. Her palms clammy, Maxine headed over, positioned herself between Avery and Claudette, and accepted the sheet of lyrics from Sandy. As the opening chords of "Winter Wonderland" filled the Christmas Corner, Sandy stood before her four employees and held her arms out on either side like a conductor. Maxine wondered how her mom and stepdad, the music snobs, would react to this moment. Some customers reacted by stopping and staring, while others continued milling about, indifferent to or perhaps familiar with this act of lunacy.

"One, two, three . . . Sleigh bells ring!" Sandy sang at the top of her lungs, swooping her arms in and out.

"Are you listening?" Claudette, Avery, and Daniel chimed right in, singing in loud unison over the backup track pouring out of the speakers. "In the lane, snow is glistening . . ."

Maxine remained frozen in horror. Maybe playing her guitar in the subway would have been preferable to this.

Avery lightly nudged her with his elbow, indicating that she should add her voice to the chorus, and Maxine felt a spark of irritation. *What a kiss-ass*, she thought, glancing over at him; true to form, he was singing with abandon, not even referring to the lyrics in his hand. Meanwhile Claudette was trilling in a beautiful soprano, practically auditioning for the opera. But thankfully Daniel was stumbling over the words — "in the snowman we can build a meadow" — and when Maxine caught his eye, he made a face. Feeling a little better, Maxine started singing along, realizing she was familiar with the lyrics from movies and the couple Christmases she'd spent at Tara's apartment. Out in the crowd, a nanny and her young charge joined in, and someone else cheered. Maxine felt a laugh building in her. Somehow the moment was so ludicrous that it was almost . . . fun. She'd forgotten the pure pleasure that came with singing; sometimes it didn't matter what the music was. As long as no one she actually *knew* was —

Oh, no.

Maxine was belting out the part about frolicking "the Eskimo way" when she spotted a face in the crowd that made her voice catch. Heath Barton was standing a few feet away, a Starbucks venti cup in one hand and wraparound shades hiding his hazel eyes. As the corner of his mouth lifted in a teasing grin, he raised his cup toward Maxine in greeting, and her face turned so hot she was sure it matched Daniel's Santa suit.

"Congrats," Heath said, strolling over to Maxine a few minutes later, once all the customers had dutifully applauded.

"You mean on surviving that?" Maxine asked, out of breath. Heath's nearness was making her pulse accelerate. She brushed her sweaty bangs off her forehead, wondering if she could duck behind the Christmas tree and pull herself together. Her elf ears felt like they might be askew.

"On getting the job, silly," Heath replied, taking a sip from his cup. "Having a good morning so far?"

Maxine blinked up at him in confusion. "Heath, it's like three-thirty."

"Is it?" Heath removed his shades and checked his Tag Heuer wristwatch. "Oh, man, whenever I wake up at noon, it throws my whole day off." He glanced up as Claudette, Avery, and Daniel passed by. "'Sup, Claudette?" he called. "Heard you got the lead in *Swan Lake*. Nice." He shot her a winning smile and then looked back at Maxine. "She's a dancer at Juilliard," he explained, lowering his voice.

Of course, Maxine thought, glancing over her shoulder at Claudette, who returned Heath's smile and said something to Avery and Daniel. Maxine noticed that both boys were watching her and Heath with interest. She knew her coworkers must have been curious about Maxine's connection to Barton's heir.

"Maxine, I need to jet — I'm having lunch with my dad's accountant at Babbo," Heath was saying, touching Maxine's shoulder to get her attention. "Lately I've been more involved with the business side of the store," he added, and motioned to the cash register. "It all comes down to bills, bills, bills in the end. You know what I mean?"

"Sort of," Maxine replied, thinking that actually it all came down to Heath's hand on her shoulder right then.

"Speaking of lunch," Heath went on, sliding down his hand from Maxine's shoulder to her arm, making her stomach jump. "We should do it sometime."

Maxine nodded, trying to keep a poker face as she imagined herself and Tara on the phone that night, giggling in a totally juvenile way over Heath's unintentional double entendre. "But I've only got half an hour," she explained. "Maybe instead we could —" She paused, wondering if it would be too forward to ask a boy about nighttime plans. She pictured herself and Heath, hands linked, strolling down Fifth Avenue and gazing into the glowing window displays as snow drifted down on them. They would stop to watch the ice skaters at Rockefeller Center and get glasses of wine at Morrell's. . . .

"No worries," Heath said, dropping his voice to a whisper. "I'll talk to Mr. Perry, pull some strings to get you more free time." He gave her a conspiratorial wink, slowly removed his hand from her arm, and turned to go while Maxine watched him, melting. "And, hey, Maxine?" Heath added, glancing back at her before he descended the staircase. "You make some elf."

Before Sandy could scold her for standing around doing nothing, Maxine hurried toward the gift wrap counter, her heart racing. Now *there* was something juicy to discuss with Tara that evening: the issue of whether or not *You make some elf* was code for *I want you*.

That week at Barton's, Heath gave Maxine and Tara endless fodder for discussion since he visited the Christmas Corner daily, always delivering a flirtatious remark ("Hot tights, Silver"), and, once, a kiss on the cheek. The kiss came after a disastrous group rendition of "Hark! the Herald Angels Sing," so when Heath unexpectedly leaned close, whispered, "Nice work," and pressed his warm lips against Maxine's skin, it felt like a reward. Trembly-kneed, Maxine took a step back and grinned up at him. Daniel, Claudette, and Avery were lingering nearby, recovering from the trauma of their performance, but Maxine was barely aware of her coworkers, or the rest of the Christmas Corner crush around her.

"I'm sorry I haven't made good on that lunch date," Heath

said, his hand lightly brushing the spot he had kissed as he moved a strand of hair off Maxine's face. "I promise I'll talk to Mr. Perry once my schedule has calmed down a little."

"You do that," Maxine replied, although she wasn't sure what exactly was keeping him so busy. After only a few days at Barton's, she'd realized that Heath didn't technically "work" — he floated, drifting from one part of the store to the other, coming and going at odd hours to conduct "market research," and chatting up the perfume counter girls to "assess employee satisfaction." But Maxine couldn't quibble; their flirtations by the Christmas tree, however brief, were still delicious oases in the midst of all those giant candy canes and shrieking children.

Though it turned out that Heath Barton wasn't the only bright spot in her existence as an elf. Those shrieking children, for instance, could actually be pretty damn cute. On her second day, Maxine had a bonding moment with a wide-eyed little girl who tugged on her hand and asked if she really worked in Santa's toy shop. "Yes, and I'll make some extras for you this year!" Maxine replied, startled by the sweetness of her own response. As the girl's face lit up, Maxine wondered if Avery hadn't been so off base after all. And though Maxine wasn't in love with gift wrapping just yet, helping frantic customers *could* be weirdly rewarding. Once she'd familiarized herself with the layout of the store, Maxine became something of an expert at digging up obscure items — from extra-large

cashmere Santa suits to the last remaining Prancer figurine —
and presenting them to people who were near tears. "Ask
Maxine" became a catchphrase among her coworkers, and
hearing those words gave Maxine a warm rush.

Surprisingly, Maxine's coworkers turned out to be another
not-so-bad aspect of the job. Despite her predilection for doing
tours jetés across the Christmas Corner, Claudette was as sweet
as her job title promised; during lunch, she and Maxine sometimes snuck downstairs to *ooh* and *ah* over new clothing
shipments and pick which pair of woolen gauchos they were
going to buy with their employee discounts. Even Avery's
boundless enthusiasm, which had irked Maxine from the start,
could be refreshing at times, especially when he volunteered to
take over cleanup duty at the end of a long, grueling day. And
Daniel's *whatever-dude* philosophy proved as comforting as
Maxine had predicted, though his tendency to take naps under
the Christmas tree when Sandy wasn't looking got annoying.

Mostly, though, Maxine was glad to have compatriots
under Sandy's tyrannical rule. One sleet-drenched morning,
when Sandy was stuck in traffic and running late, Avery offered
to head out to the corner café and pick up steaming mochas for
everyone. With some time to kill before ten, the foursome
gathered around the register with their drinks and swapped
stories about what had brought them to Barton's.

"Houston," Claudette sighed in her tinkly voice, cupping
her chin in her hands and gazing off into the distance. "I just

need to afford a plane ticket home to Houston for Christmas, and then everything will be okay."

"How so?" Maxine asked, sipping her mocha. As usual, Daniel and Avery were staring at Claudette in utter, silent devotion, as if every word she breathed were gospel.

Claudette lifted her bare shoulders, her wings fluttering behind her. "Lance," she explained. "My love. He's there, waiting for me. It's not really Christmas if we're not together."

Gag me, Maxine thought, while Daniel and Avery both looked crestfallen at this news.

"I'm feeling you on the plane ticket front," Daniel spoke up, fiddling with his Santa beard. "That, or I'll need to hitch a ride to San Diego. My parents will — no joke — assassinate me if I'm not home for Christmas. They're nuts."

Maxine nodded, thinking that she could relate, while Avery asked Daniel if that was why he moved out east in the first place.

"Not really," Daniel replied, shifting his beard back into place. "I'm a film student at The New School. I took this job because I'm making a documentary about department-store Santas. It's gonna be awesome — kind of like *Dogtown and Z-Boys*, only without skateboards."

"Uh-huh," Avery replied. Glancing at Maxine, he bit his lower lip and a dimple appeared in his left cheek, so Maxine could tell that, like her, he was trying hard not to laugh. It was odd to share a moment of connection with Avery, but then

Maxine brushed the feeling aside. Midwestern Boy may have been good-looking — in a generic, vanilla sort of way — but he was *so* not someone Maxine would even be friends with outside this job.

"What about you?" Maxine asked Avery, breaking their gaze and focusing on her mocha. "Why Barton's?"

"I'm studying acting at Tisch — you know, New York University?" Avery explained. "I figured this job would be good practice for an aspiring actor. And I'm from Illinois so —"

"Illinois?" Maxine repeated, grinning, and Avery nodded, taking a sip of his mocha. *Bingo!* she thought. Her Midwesterner radar never failed her.

Next it was Maxine's turn, but she couldn't very well say that she'd taken the position to spend time with Heath Barton. So she went the bald-faced-lie route and explained that she'd wanted a job that involved singing, since she was into music. She also mumbled something about wanting to afford a certain dress, but that reason didn't seem quite as noble as making it home for Christmas.

But at closing time on December 23, Maxine didn't care about being noble. Because that evening — the evening before their last official day — Sandy was handing out paychecks. As soon as Maxine received the flat envelope, she bid her coworkers good night and tore downstairs into the employee changing room. She had two clear goals, and they flashed before her like road signs: *Bank. Dress. Bank. Dress.* Pookie & Sebastian was still open for another thirty minutes. She was going to make this happen; she hadn't suffered for six days in vain.

The downstairs shopgirls were quietly organizing stacks of glittery clutches as Maxine thundered past them, her burnt-orange woolen peacoat flapping behind her. She was zeroing in on the double doors when Heath Barton suddenly appeared and blocked her way.

"You can't leave now," Heath told her, holding up the palm of one hand and smiling devilishly. "I forbid you."

Maxine hadn't seen Heath yet that day, and normally would have welcomed any excuse to return his playful banter. But tonight was an exception. She crossed her arms over her chest, close to pissed. "Heath, stop it. I have to be some-where."

"Not in those ears you don't," Heath shot back, his grin deepening.

"Wha — ?" Maxine touched the sides of her head to con-firm Heath's claim, and sure enough, her pointy friends were still in place. Trying not to blush, Maxine yanked them off and crammed them into her messenger bag. She could well imag-ine the sight she would have made. *Citywide police alert! There's an insane elf running up Columbus Avenue!*

"Listen, Maxine," Heath said, and he moved in close to her, so close that she could suddenly feel the warmth coming off him and smell his smoke-and-cider scent. Maxine's pulse had already been going nuts from her mad dash through

Barton's; now it shot up to an emergency-room rate. "I talked to Mr. Perry today, so we're on for lunch tomorrow," Heath continued, his voice deep and private. "I'll come pick you up around noon?"

Finally! Maxine felt a swell of anticipation as she met Heath's gaze. What a glorious way to celebrate her last day at Barton's. She hoped they'd go someplace cozy and low-lit, maybe with a fireplace and waiters serving something gross-but-fancy, like caviar on toast. It would be, quite simply, the best lunch of Maxine Silver's life. "Sounds good," she told Heath, trying to keep her tone neutral.

Heath nodded, and a look of gratitude passed over his handsome face. "Terrific," he said. "There's something I've been wanting to ask you for a long time, and, well —" He smiled and pushed a hand through his black hair. "You'll see tomorrow."

Oh . . . my . . . God. Maybe it was because The Dress was mere heartbeats away, but suddenly Maxine knew what Heath wanted to ask her. "Is it about New Year's?" she whispered. It all made sense, didn't it? Heath hadn't brought up Tara's party before, so he was clearly waiting for the two of them to be alone . . . so he could ask Maxine to be his date. Maxine felt dizzy with luck and surprise. Everything she had worked toward this week was coming together in one moment of pure joy.

Heath's mouth lifted in a half smile. "I guess, in part," he replied mysteriously. "Hey, look," he added before Maxine could press him further, and glanced up at the door frame under which he stood. "Mistletoe."

Maxine followed his gaze and, sure enough, there it was, a slender green sprig tied with a red bow, hanging innocently over Barton's entrance. On all her trips in and out of the store, Maxine had never noticed it, but then again, the boy she was dying to kiss had never been standing directly underneath it. "Oh," Maxine managed, feeling her cheeks color. Suddenly, making it to Pookie & Sebastian in time was the last thing on her mind.

"We must obey the mistletoe, right?" Heath asked teasingly. Putting one hand on Maxine's waist, he drew her close, angled his face down toward hers, and kissed her quickly on the lips. His mouth tasted like apples and she felt his stubble lightly scratch her cheek. Then Heath pulled back, grinning at her. "Sorry — you were rushing off somewhere?" he asked, and then stepped out of the way.

Face burning, heart thudding, Maxine staggered outside. The sharp night wind, carrying the scent of roasted chestnuts, whipped at her, pedestrians pushed past her, and a street musician made his saxophone wail, but Maxine noticed none of it. All she could feel was the tingling of her own lips and the heat of her skin. God, it was almost torturous to have gotten such a small taste of Heath's kisses. Maybe at lunch tomorrow, after telling her how he felt about her and asking her to Tara's party, he'd lean over the caviar and kiss her again. And then there'd be New Year's Eve: champagne corks popping, white-and-gold balloons, Heath in a suit, his hand on her lower back, his lips against her neck . . .

Now all she needed was the outfit that would make that night complete.

Maxine floated over to a Washington Mutual, deposited her check in the ATM, and then flew up Columbus to Pookie & Sebastian, where the dress waited, glowing, in the window. Maxine grabbed eagerly for the door handle, but a frosty blonde shopgirl — *my sister in sales,* Maxine thought with a flash of sympathy — began locking the door from the inside, firmly shaking her head.

"Oh, come *on!*" Maxine cried, hopping up and down. "Two seconds!" Once one has sung Christmas carols while wearing elf tights, she realized, shame wasn't really such an issue in life anymore.

Rolling her eyes, the shopgirl cracked open the door for Maxine, who rushed in and made straight for the corner rack, where — *whew* — her size was still available. She paid for the dress with her debit card, relishing the knowledge that she now had more than enough in her account to cover it. Hell, she finally had enough to buy holiday gifts for everyone. Tomorrow, she'd put her Barton's discount to good use and get perfume for her mom, cuff links for Scott, and something extra-special-glam for Tara.

"Okay, start over!" Tara exclaimed on the phone that

night. Maxine had called her, giddy and babbling, as soon as she'd left Pookie & Sebastian, but Tara had been hanging holly and had had to call back. Now, she'd caught Maxine just as she was modeling The Dress before the mirror in her bedroom.

"What do you want to hear about first — Heath or The Dress?" Maxine teased, coquettishly peeking at herself over one shoulder. Her clothes from the day were strewn across her twin bed and indigo carpet, and her We Are Scientists CD was on at full volume, drowning out her mom's and Scott's cello playing in the living room. They were rehearsing for their upcoming concert *again*.

"Duh." Tara laughed. "So he kissed you, and then he said —"

"No, *first* he said he had something to ask me, possibly related to New Year's, and then . . ." Maxine trailed off, beaming.

"Max." Tara's voice was quivery with excitement. "You know what this means, don't you? Heath *likes* you. This is *huge*. You're going to date Heath Barton!"

"I'm going to date Heath Barton," Maxine repeated softly, smiling at herself in the mirror as a thrill raced through her. "Tar, I know — can you *believe* it?"

"Well, at least I'll get to see it at my party." Tara sighed, and Maxine pictured her friend sitting on her grandparents' window seat, her chin on her knees as she watched the snow fall. Though it had been blizzarding in Oregon, it hadn't snowed in New York even once this winter. "And now you have The Dress," Tara went on. "So is your life complete?"

Is it? Maxine felt a sudden tug in the pit of her stomach. Her smile faded slightly as she studied her reflection. Was she the kind of girl who needed a dress, or shoes, or any store-bought treat to know true bliss? Since when had her winter break — her *life* — boiled down to the pursuit of material things? Maxine thought of the customers at Barton's, all hunting for what they hoped would make their Christmas complete, and an unexpected sadness washed over her. Maybe Heath had been right; everything was about bills, bills, bills, in the end. But Maxine was no longer sure if she wanted to be a part of all that.

Then Maxine glanced down at her dress, admiring how its pale gold sheen caught the light, and she shrugged off her bizarre moment of brooding. She'd have plenty of time for deep thoughts *after* Heath saw her in The Dress on New Year's Eve. For now, she could simply revel in the glory.

"Max? You there?" Tara was asking. "Did Heath just sweep into your room and, like, propose to you?"

"Ask me that tomorrow." Maxine giggled, and flopped back onto her bed, the gauzy skirt of the dress poufing up around her. "But wait — I can't call you after work, can I? It'll be Christmas Eve."

Tara groaned. "Yup. For the next forty-eight hours, I'll be

knee-deep in family duties like pretending to eat my grand-mother's turkey, keeping my cousins from opening their gifts early, making sure my uncle doesn't drink too much eggnog . . ."

"Sounds better than my non-Christmas." Maxine sighed, staring up at her tattered poster of the Strokes. "Mom and Scott are having some of their Philharmonic friends over tomorrow night to play chamber music." Maxine rolled her eyes, and knew Tara was doing the same on the other end. "Then on Christmas Day *no one* is going to be around. I guess I can spend it organizing my iTunes library."

Tara chuckled. "Oh, please. You'll be so happy after your lunch with Heath that you won't *want* to do anything but lie on your bed and stare dreamily at your Strokes poster — which I'm sure is what you're doing right now."

"Have a kickass Christmas, Tar," Maxine said, and blew a kiss into the phone. "I'll call you first thing on the twenty-sixth." Grinning, she clicked off and stretched across the bed in her gold dress. The digital clock on her bedside table told her it was almost midnight, and excitement shot through her. She was in no rush for it to be Christmas, but tomorrow couldn't come fast enough.

After managing a few hours of sleep, Maxine headed to Barton's with more energy than she'd ever had on an early work morning. But she needed every ounce of it, because that day, everyone in New York seemed to be on a mission to buy out the Christmas Corner before nightfall. In between managing the madness and slinking away to buy her holiday gifts, Maxine was caught off guard by noon's arrival. She had just enough time to change out of her elf gear and into her rhinestone-studded denim mini, mocha-colored turtleneck, and platform boots.

"Wow, you look great," Heath said when they met at the staircase. Holding his ubiquitous Starbucks cup in one hand, he put the other on Maxine's arm and gave her a kiss on the cheek, stirring up delicious memories from last night. Maxine wished Sandy had hung some mistletoe in the Corner — it seemed to be the *only* Christmas decoration not present.

"But you didn't need to change," Heath added, pulling back and winking at Maxine. "We're only going upstairs."

"We are?" Maxine asked, disappointment pricking her like a needle. *Upstairs* could only mean the third floor, which Sandy referred to as the "Cruise Wear" department — the section for those lucky few who traveled to warm climes in the winter. Curious, Maxine followed Heath up the winding staircase to the third level — and felt like she had landed on another planet. Maxine gazed around in wonder at the racks of sherbet-colored bikinis, the shelves of bejeweled flip-flops, and the tables stacked high with flowery sarongs. Unlike the level below them, this floor was hushed and empty, with nary a customer or salesperson in sight. Maxine's breath quickened. Had Heath brought her up here so they could be utterly alone? Maybe any second he'd turn to her, wrap an arm around her waist, and whisper that ever since high school, he'd been kind of in love with —

"Ever since high school," Heath spoke, and Maxine gave a start. "I've noticed that you have this rocking sense of style." Before a blushing Maxine could modestly wave him off, Heath gestured to a stack of string bikinis on a table and added, "So I figured you'd be the best girl to give me advice on these."

Maxine frowned, confusion muddying her glee. Unless Heath had some freaky cross-dressing streak, she couldn't think why he'd want the two of them to go swimsuit shopping.

Heath lifted up a pink-and-black halter, studying it closely. "This would look really hot on Julianne because she's all tan and whatnot, but do you think it's too trendy?" He shot a worried glance at Maxine. "Julianne already has all this designer stuff so I wanted to get her something more unique for Christmas, you know?"

Maxine felt a coldness seep into her limbs. *Who's Julianne?* she almost whispered, but she already knew. She knew, with a certainty that made her chest seize up, that Heath Barton had asked her here to help him pick out a bikini for his girlfriend. So *that* was what he'd been wanting to ask her for a long time. Maxine had thought she'd done away with shame but now she felt it flooding her face, consuming her completely.

"Why — um — why a bikini?" Maxine asked, hoping her voice didn't sound as shaky to Heath as it did to her ears. She felt she had to ask *something* in order to beat down the other questions rising inside her. As in: *Why did you act like you were into me, you asshole?*

"Oh, I didn't tell you?" Heath asked, now rifling through the bikinis and picking out a lemon-yellow bandeau. "My parents and I always fly down to our place in Anguilla on Christmas Eve, and this year Julianne's meeting us there. She's flying in from Aspen, so I'm sure she won't have bought a new bikini." He looked up at Maxine. "Do you like the yellow more?"

"You spend Christmas in Anguilla?" Maxine felt that as long as she kept talking, she'd manage to avoid bursting into tears of humiliation. Had she really believed — all this time —

"Family tradition," Heath replied as he examined a zebra-print two-piece. "We stay through New Year's, too, so" — he gave her a sheepish smile — "that was the other thing I wanted to ask you. I know your friend's having a party, and obviously I won't be able to make it. Can you let her know? I got her Evite but I think I deleted it by accident."

A great wave of hurt crested over Maxine. She thought of The Dress, waiting in her closet, and feared that sobbing might be around the corner. "But — but Anguilla isn't all that Christmasy," she managed in a choked voice, when what she really wanted to say was *Thanks for ruining my winter break, you bastard.* "I thought you guys would go to, like, London since your dad's British and all." She swallowed hard, willing her eyes not to tear.

Heath snorted, momentarily forgetting the bikinis.

"British? He was born in Staten Island. His real name's Charlie Barstein — oh, but don't tell anyone, 'kay?" He turned to Maxine and held up the zebra bikini. "Too much?" he asked.

Maxine shook her head, speechless. What was *too much* was her realization that everything about Barton's — from its name to its owner to its hot young heir — was phonier than the Kate Spade knockoffs sold on the street outside the store. Maxine took a step back, looking Heath up and down as if she were noticing him for the first time. In truth, the suave, sexy Heath Barton was nothing more than a spoiled little rich boy with only one true love: himself. He hadn't had a thing for her, Maxine understood. She'd been just another quick flirtation — another girl who would inflate his ego while his girlfriend was away. That was all. What a fool Maxine had been. A silly, lovestruck, elf-girl fool.

"You *kissed* me," Maxine spoke up, finding her voice and her courage at the same time. Steadier now, she met Heath's bewildered gaze. "You kissed me, but you have a girlfriend. How is that cool?"

Heath blinked at her. "Uh, hello, Maxine — mistletoe?" He said this as if she were overlooking the world's most obvious fact.

Mistletoe. Now it was anger that rushed through Maxine, quelling the threat of tears. She was sick of mistletoe and tinsel and all the trappings of the season. She was *done* with Barton's, and with the Christmas Corner. But she'd never have even been here in the first place if it weren't for Heath. At this realization, Maxine felt a fresh surge of fury.

"You know what?" she began, glaring at Heath. "It doesn't matter what bikini you get Julianne, does it? Because within a year she'll probably figure out how self-absorbed and arrogant you are, or you'll cheat on her or something, and she'll wind up returning all your meaningless gifts anyway." She took a deep breath, backing up toward the staircase as Heath watched her, slack-jawed. "So now, if you'll excuse me, I, unlike you, have a *job* to do."

Fuming, Maxine whirled around and started down the staircase. Heath remained silent and immobile behind her, but just as she reached the second level, she heard him call out to her.

"Hang on," Heath said, leaning over the banister with the bikinis still in hand. Maxine was pleased to see that he looked ruffled and out of sorts, and hoped some of what she'd said had sunk in. Then Heath spoke again. "You never told me which one you liked better."

Maxine stared up at him in disbelief. "The zebra," she finally replied. "It's kind of expensive-tacky — like you." With that, she stormed into the Christmas Corner, promptly bumping into Avery, who was carrying a stack of Santa suits to the cash register.

"Whoa, is everything all right?" Avery asked, raising his eyebrows at her.

Ugh. The last thing she needed now was Avery's sympathy — which was probably all an act anyway. "Oh, like you care," Maxine snapped, brushing past him without a second thought.

For the first time in her Barton's career, Maxine was grateful to change into her elf costume. She was shaking with anger, continually replaying the ugly scene with Heath in her head, so it was a relief to throw herself back into work, even if that work involved tearing apart two grown women who were wrestling over a chocolate snowman, and fumbling through a performance of "The Little Drummer Boy."

The Corner grew more crowded as the afternoon progressed. It didn't help that Claudette danced off early to catch her plane to Houston, hugging everyone and promising to stay in touch but clearly psyched to be getting out of there. By the time seven o'clock — the normal closing hour — rolled around, Maxine was starving (she'd never eaten), sweaty, and ready to settle down for a long winter's nap. When Sandy rounded up her, Daniel, and Avery for an impromptu meeting, Maxine hoped that it was to tell them they were free to leave, despite the fact that the place was still a mob scene.

But Sandy delivered the opposite news. "The word's come down from Mr. Perry: We're staying open until nine," she announced grimly, peering at her employees over her clipboard. "I expect each of you to remain here and help close up."

"Dude, no can do — I'm catching a nine-o'clock flight at JFK," Daniel spoke up, looking more alert than Maxine had ever seen him. "I assumed we'd get off early on our last day, and —"

Before Sandy could bark at Daniel, Avery spoke up. "I can stay, but just until eight," he offered, removing his boxy Nutcracker hat and running a hand through his blond hair. "There's something I need to —"

"I get it, I get it," Sandy snapped, putting one hand on her hip. "What can I expect on Christmas Eve?" She shot a glance at Maxine. "And you, Elf?"

Maxine opened her mouth, ready to invent some fib about catching a plane, train, or automobile — but then realized she didn't want to. The truth was, she had no place to be on Christmas Eve and, in a twisted way, closing up the Corner would be preferable to enduring a lame night at home: live chamber music emanating from the living room, her mom and Scott all over each other, Maxine locked in her bedroom, seething over Heath Barton . . .

"I'll stay," Maxine said, squaring her shoulders.

"Well, it's the least you can do considering you took a long lunch today," Sandy replied, by way of thanking her.

"Maxine, righteous of you to stay the course," Daniel said, giving her a good-bye kiss on the cheek and knocking fists with Avery. "We'll be forever grateful."

Maxine shrugged. "I'm a Hanukkah kind of girl anyway,

so it's not like I've got big Christmas plans," she said matter-of-factly. Then she wished Daniel well and headed for the gift wrap counter, where Sandy was beckoning to her and Avery.

For the next hour, as Maxine worked the Christmas Corner alongside Avery, she felt some of her fury ebbing away. She and Avery actually made a solid team, he handing her a tube of wrapping paper just when she was reaching for it, she passing him the scissors before he could ask for them. It was Avery who kept the maniacal customers calm while Maxine hunted for hard-to-find items; once, after managing to quiet a bellowing grandpa-type with the right snow globe, the two of them exchanged a relieved grin, and Maxine felt a pang of regret over how she'd dismissed him earlier. Avery may have been studying acting in school, but, as Maxine observed him across the store — patiently listening to a panicked mom, saluting on command for a group of giggling girls — she realized that the sparkle in his blue-gray eyes and the warmth in his smile were entirely genuine.

Maxine was kneeling beneath the gift wrap counter, retrieving a Barton's box and wondering if she should apologize to him, when Avery himself leaned over the counter.

"It's, um, almost eight," he said awkwardly, turning his boxy Nutcracker hat around and around in his hands. "I should — you know —"

"It's okay," Maxine said, getting to her feet. "Have a merry —"

"So, um, I guess I'll see you," Avery said abruptly, lifting one hand in farewell and backing off in a hurry.

He hates me, Maxine decided, watching him go. She wished she'd at least told him that he was maybe the only guy who could pull off looking that good in a Nutcracker costume. But now, considering he was headed home to Illinois for Christmas, she'd probably never see him again. Melancholy settled over Maxine like a dusting of snow, and she focused again on the line of impatient customers.

At five to nine, Sandy finally granted Maxine her freedom and, looking as though she were in pain, thanked her for a job well done. Instead of feeling footloose and festive, though, Maxine found herself fighting down a lump in her throat. Slowly, she changed out of her elf clothes for the very last time, slipped on her coat, hat, and scarf, and scooped up her messenger bag full of holiday gifts. She made her way through the silent ground level, and the security guard locked the door behind her as she stepped outside. *Good-bye, Barton's.*

Maxine stood by herself on Fifth Avenue, breathing in the wintry air. As she drew her coat collar up, she lifted her eyes to the giant twinkling snowflake, which, in the nighttime gloom, suddenly seemed very lonely. *Or maybe that's just me,* Maxine thought, swallowing hard. Rather than heading for home, she turned and began meandering down the empty avenue, passing the tall, glamorous facades of Bergdorf Goodman, Louis Vuitton, Harry Winston, and Bulgari. The stores' holiday windows — white lights twined around silvery branches, elaborately designed dolls arranged in scenes from *A Christmas Carol* — were incongruously bright against the darkness. Maxine thought she heard laughter and the sound of glasses clinking coming from a window high above her, but she couldn't place the source of the merriment. A lone taxicab shot past, startling her; its windows were rolled down, and the song "All Alone on Christmas" blasted out into the night.

"The cold wind is blowin' and the streets are getting dark . . . nobody ought to be all alone on Christmas."

The song capped everything off; Maxine stopped in the middle of Fifth Avenue, buried her face in her mittened hands, and surrendered to the tears that had been building ever since she'd learned the truth about Heath that afternoon. As the warm, salty drops fell, Maxine, who didn't cry all that often, let herself wallow in self-pity. She'd had the day from hell, but this moment was worse than anything that had happened back at Barton's — because she felt like the only person alive not celebrating somewhere. The shops, the decorations, and the music were not for her. Standing in the heart of her hometown — in a city packed with so many interesting and quirky people who celebrated all varieties of holidays — Maxine Silver had somehow never felt so adrift.

"I don't think Sandy would approve."

A voice at her side and a hand on her arm made Maxine

glance up and instinctively tug her bag against her. But the person standing beside her was not a Christmas Eve mugger. It was Avery Prince.

"I mean, that's not much holiday cheer you're showing, is it?" Avery clarified, and though his tone was playful, concern darkened his blue-gray eyes.

"Oh, um, I guess not." Maxine sniffled, rubbing the tears off her cheeks. She wished he hadn't seen her crying. But what was he even *doing* here? Maxine blinked, noticing that Avery was holding two cups topped with whipped cream, and wearing a fur-lined bomber jacket over a navy-blue sweater and corduroys. It was the first time Maxine had ever seen Avery out of his Nutcracker gear and, in spite of herself, her heart skipped a beat. There had been something adorable about Avery in costume, but seeing him now, the word that came to mind was *beautiful.* His high cheekbones, corn-silk hair, the dimple in his left cheek when he smiled . . . how had Maxine never picked up on it before?

"I'm sorry if I startled you — I stopped by Barton's first," Avery was explaining. "But then I saw you standing down here, so . . ." He lifted one shoulder, his smile shy.

Maxine's head spun as she tried to piece together what Avery was saying. "You . . . you were looking for *me?*" she stammered. "But why — I thought you were going home —"

Avery shook his head, extending one of those cups toward

Maxine. "I didn't have time to make travel arrangements this year. Flights to Chicago book up so fast." He paused, and his eyes swept over Maxine's face, making her breath catch a little. "Here," he added softly. "You seem like you could use some hot cocoa."

"No kidding," Maxine said gratefully, accepting the cup from Avery. She was reminded of the morning he had brought in mochas for the group; he really *was* a thoughtful guy. Maxine blew on the steaming surface, then took a sip. The rich, sweet liquid warmed her to the core and seemed to sate her hunger. Avery, too, was sipping his drink, and as he and Maxine looked at each other over their respective brims, Maxine could feel herself start to smile.

Without a word, the two of them turned and slowly began walking south on Fifth, their elbows touching each time they lifted their cups to their lips. Whenever this happened, Maxine felt a tingle move up her arm, and she wondered if Avery was feeling the same thing. As they walked on, with the lights from the store windows illuminating their path, they began to talk, their breath forming clouds on the air. They laughed over Sandy's clipboard, dissected Daniel's spaciness, and debated whether or not Claudette could ever be clumsy. Somehow discussing Barton's with Avery made Maxine feel worlds better, and she was surprised to learn that even he had some issues with the job.

"So how did you do it?" Maxine asked him with genuine

interest as they approached Rockefeller Center. "You always seemed so . . . glad to be there."

Avery glanced at her with a half smile. "Trust me, Maxine, I had my down moments, just like you. But I try to make the best of things. I know, I know." He laughed as Maxine wrinkled her nose. "Cue the corniness, right? But I never really *minded* Barton's. After all, if I didn't work there, I wouldn't have met —" Avery paused and drank from his cocoa again, his face coloring.

Me? Maxine thought, her stomach giving a jump. She was still feeling too unsteady to pose such a bold question, so instead she simply nodded, clutching her cocoa cup.

"But the commercialism of this time of year does get to me," Avery added thoughtfully, as he and Maxine turned in to Rockefeller Center. The red, gold, and green flags flapped in the wind, the tree glowed, and the golden statue of Prometheus watched over the pure-white rink, on which only a smattering of skaters zipped about. "Everyone's so hung up on buying stuff . . ." As they reached the ledge that overlooked the rink, Avery gazed down at the skaters, the light from below casting shadows on his profile.

Maxine glanced at Avery, surprised that he had echoed her thoughts from the night before. Maybe she and Midwestern Boy had more in common than Maxine had first thought. "So what's the alternative?" Maxine teased, playing devil's advocate. She gave Avery a nudge in the side, thinking how much more relaxed she was around him, as opposed to, say, Heath Barton. "A holiday without gifts? Horrors!"

Avery turned to her, smiling and shaking his head. "Well, gifts can also be, like . . . moments instead of things, you know?" he asked, then bit his lip. "Does that make sense?"

Like this moment, Maxine caught herself thinking, and a warmth that had nothing to do with the hot cocoa spread through her body. Suddenly she felt something wet land on her cheek, and then her nose, and Maxine tilted her head up, laughing. Glistening white flakes were swirling down from the sky; the first snowfall of the year. From the skating rink below, Maxine heard people break out into cheers of appreciation.

Avery, too, looked up and laughed, and then glanced back at Maxine. "Is New York City always this postcard-perfect in the winter?" he asked, setting down his cocoa cup and attempting to catch the dancing white dots in his hands.

"We try," Maxine replied, blinking snowflakes off her lashes, and realizing that Avery's wide-eyed enthusiasm wasn't getting on her nerves this time. It was actually kind of fun to experience the city with a non-native. "Wait," Maxine added, remembering something Avery had said earlier. "If you weren't going back to Illinois tonight, why did you have to leave early?"

"Oh." Avery looked down abruptly, his cheeks flushing again, and Maxine felt a sudden wave of nervousness that colored her own face. "I, um, well, now that you ask . . . I was going to get you something," he said.

"You were?" Maxine asked breathlessly, and then pointed to her empty cocoa cup on the ledge. "You mean . . . this?"

Avery shook his head, still studying the snow-dusted ground. "Nah — I got those after the original plan didn't work out." Slowly, Avery raised his eyes until he met Maxine's gaze. "I went to Lincoln Center to get us . . . tickets. Tickets to the New York Philharmonic's concert next week." He let out a big breath, looking crestfallen. "But it was sold out."

Maxine clapped a hand over her mouth, unable to stop her burst of laughter. What were the chances? "Avery, you didn't need to do that!" she exclaimed, feeling as dizzy and carefree as the snowflakes tumbling around her. When he shook his head politely, Maxine clarified. "No, I mean, you *really* didn't have to do that. I know it's random, but my mom and stepdad are *in* the Philharmonic. They're going to play in that concert, and can totally get us tickets." Normally Maxine wouldn't have been excited by the prospect of one of her mom's concerts, but the thought of going with Avery, of seeing him again outside Barton's, made her pulse flutter.

"That is exceptionally cool," Avery declared, his face lighting up with relief. "You must get to hear amazing music all the time."

"Eh," Maxine replied, making a so-so motion with her hand. "Classical's not my favorite." When Avery nodded in agreement, Maxine added, "So what made you think of the Philharmonic then?"

Avery grinned, lifting one shoulder. "Well, you mentioned once you loved music. So I figured you'd enjoy something more, I don't know, peaceful after all that Christmas carol *mishegas* we had to go through." He rolled his eyes for emphasis.

"Um . . . what did you just say?" Maxine asked, wondering if the snowfall had affected her hearing.

"Mishegas?" Avery repeated, grinning. "You know, it's Yiddish. It means craziness or whatever —"

"I know," Maxine cut him off, now thoroughly confused. "It's my Grandma Rose's favorite expression but —"

"My grandma's, too," Avery said matter-of-factly, brushing his blond hair back off his forehead.

"But Avery —" Maxine sputtered as the implications of his words hit home. "I thought you were — don't you celebrate Christmas?"

Avery shook his head, his eyes sparkling. "I *like* Christmas a lot, but I guess you'd say I'm more of a Hanukkah kind of guy." He stuck his hands in his pockets and shrugged. "Happy Hanukkah, by the way — even though it's been over for a couple of days now."

Maxine's lips parted in amazement. Avery Prince was . . . *Jewish?* She thought about how isolated she'd felt in all that Christmas madness, when all along, of all people . . . And suddenly, it made perfect sense that Avery had met her on lonesome Fifth Avenue, and now stood with her in a quiet, sparkling Rockefeller Center. He didn't have Christmas Eve plans, either. She wasn't so alone after all.

"What are you thinking, Maxine Silver?" Avery asked, flashing her an intrigued smile and taking a step closer to her.

"Oh . . . nothing." Maxine laughed, looking up at him. "Just that I'm never going to assume something about anyone ever again."

Avery nodded, holding her gaze, and then his expression turned serious — intense. Through the steady snowfall, Maxine watched him study her, and her heart tapped against her ribs. "What are *you* thinking?" she volleyed back at him.

"Just that . . ." Avery reached over and brushed a snowflake off the tip of Maxine's nose. "When you're not dressed like an elf, you're even more beautiful."

Maxine felt her face grow hotter than it ever had under Heath Barton's gaze. Heath's compliments had been flip and fleeting, but she could sense the earnestness behind Avery's words. And for once, Maxine was speechless. All she could do was step forward and meet Avery as he was stepping closer to her. No mistletoe was necessary; the moment alone told them what to do. Maxine let her eyes drift shut as Avery lowered his face and kissed her, soft and slow. *I'm kissing the Nutcracker Prince*, Maxine thought as she felt Avery's warm lips claim hers, but instead of laughing, she kissed him back, savoring every second. The way their mouths fit together, the way Avery's arms went around her waist right as hers went around his neck, seemed to cancel out any kiss — or any moment — she'd shared with Heath Barton.

"You idiot." Maxine sighed when they broke apart, resting her fingers against Avery's lips. "Why didn't you do that *days* ago?"

Avery laughed, shaking his head. "Maxine, I thought you had written me off from the start. When I met you, you were so, I don't know, sassy and funny, and that was what I liked about you, but it also made me nervous. . . ." He glanced down, clearly embarrassed. "And then you were always chatting with Heath Barton, so I figured . . ."

"You figured wrong," Maxine whispered, standing on her toes to kiss Avery's cheek. Heath seemed very far away now, and not only because he was off in Anguilla. Maxine's crush on him felt distant, faded around the edges, like an old photograph from high school.

Holding hands, Avery and Maxine turned and left Rockefeller Center and, as the snow continued to drift down, wound their way toward Maxine's apartment building. When they reached the green awning on 79th Street, they lingered on the corner, far from the curious gaze of Maxine's doorman. Avery had to head back downtown to his NYU dorm but first there were matters to discuss.

"If you're around tomorrow," Avery murmured, lacing his fingers through Maxine's, his warm breath tickling her ear. "Would you be up for a movie and Chinese food?"

"Of course." Maxine laughed. It seemed her iTunes library would have to wait, she realized with a swell of happiness. "The Jewish tradition. What else is there to do on Christmas, right?"

"Well . . . this, for one," Avery whispered. Gently, he lifted Maxine's chin and started kissing her once more. Only this time their kiss was fierce and deep and passionate, and Maxine's hands were in Avery's hair and he was clutching the back of her coat to draw her in closer, and Maxine wondered if it was possible to faint from wanting a boy this badly. Midwestern Boy — who knew? Maxine would have never guessed that someone from Illinois could kiss so well, or be so effortlessly sexy.

"So speaking of plans," Maxine murmured against Avery's lips, smiling. "If *you're* around on New Year's Eve, I know of a certain fabulous party . . ." Her heart soared as she thought of The Dress; now *here* was a boy worth wearing it for.

"I'm there," Avery replied, playfully tugging Maxine's cloche hat down over her eyes.

As she and Avery started kissing again, under the falling snow and the light from a tinsel-wrapped lamppost, Maxine suddenly felt like the whole city — from the shimmery decorations on the storefronts to the Christmas carols drifting down from an apartment window above — was all for her tonight. All for *them*. And that realization, combined with the feel of Avery's arms around her, was as sweet and warm and satisfying as a holiday song.

* * * * * * *

HAVE YOURSELF
A MERRY LITTLE
BREAKUP

By Hailey Abbott

* * * * * * *

"Absolutely not," Aria declared when Marcus slowed his walk outside of Abercrombie, nearly getting them run over by the Christmas Eve mall traffic. "If I go in there, I'm going to buy myself those flare-leg jeans, and I swore I wouldn't buy anything else until after Christmas. I might need to go on a shopping strike until summer."

Marcus laughed, his blue eyes gleaming. "Oh, come on, Aria," he teased. "Don't be such a stick-in-the-mud."

Aria made a face. "I can't help it. Plus we *are* here on business, remember?"

Marcus nodded. "Locate gift, purchase gift, present gift to Emily," he recited robotically, then smiled down into Aria's upturned face. "I know."

"Good," Aria said, leading the way through the packed mall. Racing past J. Crew, she caught a quick glimpse of their reflections in the glass storefront. Though Aria was tall — nearly five foot seven — Marcus still towered over her. They made a striking pair, what with her skin the color of dark coffee, and Marcus's the pale hue of cedar wood. While Marcus's hair was reddish-brown and straight, Aria's was dark brown, and though she usually wore it in a row of braids, today it fell to her shoulders in a riot of curls.

Not for the first time, Aria wondered if people assumed she and Marcus were a couple. But they weren't. Marcus's true love, his girlfriend of three years, was Aria's best friend, Emily. And Aria's heart belonged to Jason, the captain of their high school football team. Aria, Emily, Jason, and Marcus had been a formidable foursome, double-dating every Saturday night, until Emily, who was a year older than the others, had left for college in September. Aria missed her best friend every day, and she knew Marcus felt the same way.

It was six o'clock on December 24th, and Garden State Plaza mall was bursting with manic Christmas energy. A brass band played carols to the crowd, while little kids cried out for toys. The air smelled sweet like sugar cookies. "Silver Bells" echoed through the gleaming corridors, drowning out the sales pitches of vendors in their stalls. Aria couldn't stop looking at all the stressed-out, angry people pushing through the crowds, bags hung over their arms, determined to somehow find the perfect gift.

"Check out the two ladies by the perfume counter," she told Marcus, tugging on his elbow.

"The ones who are about to claw each other's eyes out for that last gift set?" Marcus asked.

"I don't understand." Aria shook her head in disbelief. "It's Christmas Eve, and everyone looks like they want to kill each other."

"Happy freaking holidays," Marcus said, but he was grinning as he said it.

"I don't know why, but it all cracks me up," Aria said with a laugh. "Everyone stresses out so much, but then it all turns out great in the end. You know?"

"You're so the eternal optimist," Marcus said as they passed Quiksilver, American Eagle, and Victoria's Secret, with its mannequins in Santa hats and bikini briefs. Then Marcus came to a stop outside a small, independent café, which boasted less of a crowd than the Starbucks across the way, and had cozy-looking couches. It was like an oasis in the middle of so much frantic Christmas cheer.

"I can't deal with any of this without fortification," Marcus explained. "Wanna grab us a seat?"

Aria opened her mouth to protest — they were here on a mission — but she realized she could do with a small pick-me-up. She and Marcus headed inside, and Aria settled herself at a small table near the glass window. In its reflection, she could see Marcus up at the counter, charming the barista girls with that easy grin of his. She shook her head affectionately.

Marcus's swagger caused girls to flutter around him without his even trying, which was why Emily had entrusted him to Aria for the year. Emily was at Oberlin, all the way in Ohio, so she couldn't return home for visits all that often. And while she knew that Marcus could be trusted, the girls who fixated on him could *not*. It was up to Aria to keep an eye on things for her.

Aria rested her chin in her hand, thinking of her best friend. Thank God Emily was coming back for break — now everything could go back to normal. Aria, Marcus, and Jason had spent most of that autumn commiserating over the fact that Emily had abandoned them. Their threesome had seemed empty somehow. And though Emily's break had started in mid-December, she'd spent the past couple of weeks at her new friend Erin's house. She'd be arriving home tonight, in time for Christmas Eve.

The good news was, college kids had something like six weeks off for break, so Aria was sure she'd be able to pretend that Emily was actually home for good.

"Caramel apple cider," Marcus announced, plunking two heavy mugs on the table. "Can you think of anything more Christmasy?"

"Eggnog?" Aria offered after a moment, reaching for a mug.

"Na-sty" Marcus retorted. "I don't know how my parents can drink that stuff."

"*I* happen to enjoy it," Aria said. "Especially when my mom isn't paying attention and I can slip a little rum in. Just a little bit, though. For that extra kick."

"Aria Jones, I'm shocked and appalled," Marcus said,

smiling to show he wasn't either of those things. "I had no idea you were such a bad girl."

Aria laughed. If only. She wouldn't even know how to *start* to be a bad girl. She'd always been Ms. Straight-A, Type-A. "That's where Emily comes in," she said. "Remember?"

Marcus nodded, a faraway look in his eyes. A sadness passed over his face then, and Aria guessed he was remembering scenes from the last summer the four of them had all spent together. It had been Emily who'd decided to drive to Atlantic City to skinny-dip at nine-thirty on a Tuesday night. And Emily who had flung off her sundress and waded right in, while Aria, steadfast in shorts and flip-flops, just got her toes wet as the boys hooted them on.

Aria shook away the memory of sand and the hot, close night. She picked up her drink and took a careful sip, wary of burning her tongue.

"It's *almost* perfect," Marcus said very seriously, tasting his. "Almost, but not quite."

"Mr. Perfectionist strikes again," Aria teased him. Marcus starred in all the school musicals, and was known for rehearsing and rehearsing until he got his role just so.

"Look who's talking!" Marcus shot back. "In any case, I have a solution to the drink problem. And it might help your attitude, too." He picked up the cinnamon shaker and brandished it at her. "A bit of cinnamon sugar should do the trick."

"Careful!" Aria warned him at once. "In case you didn't notice, I'm rocking the winter white today." She gestured to her snow-colored turtleneck sweater.

He shook the shaker at her, and Aria shrieked, leaping up from her seat. Marcus was after her in a flash, threatening her with a cloud of cinnamon. Aria ducked behind a muffin display case and might have stayed there all night, had the manager not intervened and suggested — strongly — that Aria and Marcus either take their roughhousing somewhere else, or sit down. The manager was an older guy, who obviously didn't think Marcus was as cute as his two wide-eyed barista girls did.

Giggling madly, Aria and Marcus chose Option Number Two and sat down.

"Just trust me," Marcus said as if he were doing Aria a huge favor, shaking the canister over her drink.

Feeling flushed and silly, Aria tasted her drink again. "Delicious!" she pronounced with a flourish.

"Of course it is." Marcus leaned back in his chair. "I know what I'm doing."

Aria rolled her eyes and, after a few moments to savor the tart and now perfectly sweetened brew, stood up. "Okay," she said. "Playtime is over. We have to find a gift."

Marcus sighed as if she'd suggested they start their homework.

"For Emily?" Aria prompted him. "Remember? Your girlfriend? Christmas? Which is *tomorrow*, by the way?"

"Okay, okay." Marcus got to his feet, and waved Aria in front of him.

Aria couldn't believe Marcus's slacking off. She'd had a great gift for Emily since mid-October, and one for Jason since November. Christmas shopping was one of Aria's favorite things — hello, it was the reason Marcus had asked her to help him out in the first place. It was *appalling* to hear that the boy had nothing to give the girlfriend he hadn't laid eyes on since Thanksgiving. Aria didn't understand guys sometimes. They were so casual about important stuff, and then, the next thing you knew, they were having strong emotions about the strangest things, like ice hockey statistics. Even the worst boyfriend in the world had to know that a Christmas present was, like, *required*, right?

But as they went from store to store, Marcus was still doing his apathetic thing. Everything Aria held up as a potential gift for Emily made him sigh. And shrug. And look bored.

"You need to get it together," Aria told him in J. Crew. "We're seeing Em in like, two hours, and you have nothing for her!"

"Whatever." Marcus shrugged.

"*Whatever?*" Aria echoed. "Marcus, what's gotten into you?"

"I can't deal," Marcus replied. It was the most he'd said since they'd left the café. And then he started talking faster, so Aria couldn't get a word in. "I don't know what she wants. You talk to her more than I do anyway. Whatever you pick out will be fine, I'm sure. I'll go get the car — the traffic is insane, so I'll meet you out by the back entrance of Borders. Okay? Thanks, Aria. This is exactly why you rule."

And just like that, he turned around and took off, leaving Aria gaping after him.

Okay, Marcus, she thought, so mad she couldn't even see the display of skinny corduroys in front of her, *how about you just explain to Emily why you don't have anything for her, because it's not* my *job to find her gift from* you!

Aria took a deep breath. She knew Marcus was a thoughtful guy. He'd never do anything to hurt Emily. He was probably just worked up about seeing Emily again.

Wandering back out into the main corridor, Aria shoved her hands into her jeans pockets and frowned into the window displays. She just wanted everything to be perfect when Emily got home. She wanted things to be the way they had always been.

Just then, her eye was caught by a store window. There, nestled around the black velvet neck of a mannequin, was a necklace of delicate gold loops. Aria found herself grinning.

Emily would love it. Marcus would look like the most attentive boyfriend who ever lived. Emily could even wear it to her own party tonight.

Emily's family threw a big, formal affair every Christmas Eve. There was a Christmas punch that usually ended up spiked, and, when it got close to midnight, dancing. Aria felt a tremor of anticipation.

I'm going to be late if I don't get my butt in gear, she realized with a glance at her watch. Aria was never late. It was like her trademark. Purposeful now, she marched into the store and asked one of the clerks to help her liberate the necklace from the mannequin, and then eyed the rest of the merchandise while the salesgirl wrapped the necklace. *It's not going to be like one of* my *wrapping jobs*, Aria thought with a smile, *but it will have to do.*

Aria trailed her fingers across a display table heaped with cashmere items at reduced prices. A blue scarf caught her attention, and she smiled as she thought about how good it would look on Marcus. It would make his eyes look even bluer.

Aria shook away the image and laughed out loud to herself. What was she thinking? Marcus wasn't hers to shower with presents, particularly not presents that showed off his eyes. God.

Jason was the boy she liked to shop for, even if he generally preferred football-related gifts. Aria was *so* not sporty, but Jason was so funny and vibrant and popular — and such a good kisser — that Aria was able to ignore their differences.

Aria dug into her satchel purse and pulled out her wallet. *I'll get it anyway.* The soft cashmere scarf would go to Jason. Marcus and Aria didn't exchange presents. Sometimes they bought each other a latte or, as before, apple cider, but that was all.

Aria thought about the night ahead, and practically wriggled in delight. She felt as if she'd been waiting forever for Christmas Eve to come and finally it was here. She couldn't wait to just kick back and start celebrating with her favorite people.

And those weird thoughts about Marcus would subside, she was sure, as soon as she was standing under the mistletoe with Jason, Marcus and Emily kissing at their side.

By the time she made it home — Marcus had dragged his feet through the mall, but the boy could drive like the wind when it suited him — Aria had very little time to get ready.

Her fingers were trembling a little — from nerves? she wondered — as she pulled her mass of tight curls back with a wide satin headband, and then tamed them into a bun that sat high on her head. Taking a deep breath, she climbed into the dress she'd bought at H & M. It was strapless and a rich, inviting velvet — a dark burgundy shade that made Aria's dark skin glow. She slipped in her favorite citrine earrings, applied lip gloss, and —

"Aria!" Her mother's voice floated up the staircase. "Jason's here!"

Aria smiled, eager to see her boyfriend. As she headed down the stairs, she spotted him in the family room near the Christmas tree. Aria's father had brought the pine home with him that Friday, and they'd spent all weekend decking the halls. The Jones family went all out for Christmas. Aria and her two little sisters loved wrapping the pine garlands around the banisters, setting up their mother's crèche, and carefully unwrapping all the delicate ornaments. There were stockings hung over the stone fireplace and tinsel draped from the exposed beams in the ceiling. Aria's mother had set up an illuminated sleigh and reindeer on the front porch. Aria could see the lights twinkling through the front windows as she came down the steps. The house smelled like pine and sugar, and the tree gleamed, laden with brightly colored ornaments and sparkling lights, with a mass of vivid presents beneath.

Aria gave a happy sigh.

Jason was all done up himself, as though he were one of the presents. He was wearing a sleek gray suit with a green tie. Though Aria saw Jason every day, she still couldn't get over how, well, *hot* he was. Though his skin was fair, his dark hair and dark eyes were the color of rich milk chocolate. When he looked up and saw Aria, it was like all that chocolate melted.

"Wow," he breathed.

"Merry Christmas," Aria whispered, walking toward him as her mom hurried away, saying she wanted to give them time alone, and had baking to supervise anyway. Aria felt grateful that her mom was understanding when it came to boyfriend stuff.

"You're so beautiful," Jason said, pulling Aria close and kissing her. Once, then twice. His lips were warm and soft. Sweetly familiar.

"You look pretty good yourself," Aria said.

They shared another kiss, but then Aria pulled back and moved away to rummage under the tree.

"Here," she said, presenting Jason with two wrapped packages.

"I brought you your gift, too," Jason said, producing a small box from his suit pocket. "Baby, I've been dying to give it to you — for months!"

Aria felt a rush of gratitude that *her* boyfriend obviously hadn't waited until the last minute to get her something. Inside the tiny box was a delicate silver star locket, nestled on a downy white pillow. It was beautiful, and Aria sighed, tracing its shape with her fingers.

"I saw that and knew it had to be yours," Jason told her. "It's so pretty, just like you." His eyes were so bright and intense that Aria had to look away. She felt something strange and twisted bloom inside herself, and just as she started to name the feeling, guilt swamped her and she thrust it from her mind.

"Open yours," she said instead, giving him a gentle shove.

He was as psyched about the new PlayStation game as she'd anticipated, and gave her a quick kiss. Then Aria watched as he opened the other box and pulled out the blue scarf. Aria bit her lip, studying the scarf on Jason. It didn't suit his coloring at all.

"Aria, baby, thank you," Jason said softly, hanging the scarf around his neck. "I love it."

It wasn't that the blue looked *bad,* she thought. It just . . . wasn't quite right. She frowned, thinking again that the blue would have looked very natural on Marcus.

As Jason helped her fasten the silver locket around her neck, Aria felt the smooth metal against her throat like some kind of chastisement. Something was going on with her. Why couldn't she fully appreciate this romantic moment? It didn't make any sense.

What she really needed, she decided as she shrugged into her winter coat, was some long-overdue time with Emily.

After all, if anyone could fix it, whatever *it* was, her best friend could.

Emily opened the front door just as Jason and Aria arrived, and for a second, everyone froze.

Behind Emily, the front hall of her house glowed with multicolored lights and the sounds of so many people making merry. And Emily was framed in the doorway, wearing a strapless black dress Aria had never seen before, as well as the necklace Aria had picked out for her a few hours earlier. As Aria had known it would, the necklace suited Emily to a T; it complemented her curly strawberry-blonde hair and wide green eyes. But though the necklace was familiar, something about *Emily* wasn't. Maybe it was the new dress, or the way she wore her hair pinned back, or . . . Aria didn't know. But her silly/crazy/hilarious best friend suddenly seemed very composed and glamorous. Mature.

"Nice of you guys to finally show up," Emily said, feigning annoyance. Then, unable to control herself, she squealed and threw her arms around Aria.

"I'm so glad you're home!" Aria whooped, hugging Emily back, hard.

Jason kissed Emily on the cheek and announced he was off to find Marcus, leaving the two girls to catch up. Emily pulled the heavy door shut, and linked her arm through Aria's as they dodged the party to find a quiet spot in the kitchen.

"Ms. Aria Jones," Emily said, her green eyes lighting up. "You're even hotter than you were at Thanksgiving."

Aria rolled her eyes. "It's the dress," she said, gesturing to her velvety front. "It creates this whole illusion of extreme fabulousness."

"It's not the dress," Emily said with a knowing look that Aria didn't entirely understand.

"Anyway, like you're one to talk!" Aria swept her best friend up and down with a critical look. "Apparently no one explained the concept of the Freshman Fifteen to you. You know, about how you're supposed to *gain* fifteen pounds?"

"I can't understand how anyone can eat cafeteria food," Emily said, wrinkling her freckled nose. "Everything's fried, or has been *sitting* for days — yuck." She shuddered dramatically, making them both laugh. Being with Emily was so familiar, so easy. Aria could feel them clicking back into that effortless synchronized space they'd spent most of their lives in.

"Come on," Emily said. "There's some very special egg-nog with your name all over it."

"I missed you," Aria told Emily with a contented sigh. "No one else understands my need for nog the way you do."

"Always," Emily assured her. She motioned for Aria to stay put, and snuck over to the big bar her parents had set up. Aria kept a look out as Emily doctored two glasses of the thick, creamy drink, and then the two of them giggled together as they retreated to the den. The boys could fend for themselves a while longer.

"You wouldn't believe the craziness at school these days," Aria told Emily when they were settled on the love seat in the small, cozy room with the door shut behind them. "For one thing, Cassandra Higgins finally broke up with Sam Parish."

"That only took six years," Emily said with a snort. "He hasn't been faithful since junior high."

"Tell me about it," Aria said, sipping her drink. "It's so scandalous."

"It's so high school," Emily said with a shrug. But she flashed Aria a wicked smile. "Want to see something *truly* scandalous?"

"Uh, sure," Aria said, feeling a prickle of doubt.

"You have to promise not to freak out," Emily said, still smiling. "And you *cannot* tell my mother!"

"I can't believe you would even bring that up. I told her you tried a cigarette that *one time* because I was worried about you, and what did I know? I was in the sixth grade!"

"Promise," Emily ordered.

"Of course I promise," Aria said, rolling her eyes.

Practically vibrating with excitement, Emily set down her drink, turned, and unzipped the side of her dress, letting it fall open so Aria could see the large, intricate tattoo that spread across the small of her back. It was a Celtic cross. Aria supposed it was beautiful. It was just so . . . big.

"I can't believe you got it without telling me!" Aria whispered. And clearly Emily had gotten it some time ago, since it didn't look red or scabby.

"Some girls on my hall and I all just decided to go one night," Emily said, zipping herself back up. She caught sight of Aria's face and sighed. "I wasn't *deliberately* not telling you, silly. I did it, and then I thought I'd surprise you with it. Pretty cool, right?"

"Very cool," Aria said. She almost believed it.

After Emily was summoned to tend to some relatives from out of town, Aria went to find Jason. She wandered through the party, passing Emily's grandparents and cousins, stopping to say hello, loving the way the different generations blended so easily. Aria breathed in the positive vibe, and any weirdness she felt about Emily's tattoo evaporated.

It wasn't like the tattoo was *that* surprising, after all. Emily probably would have gotten a nose ring if she wasn't still afraid of her very strict mother's reaction. Aria just couldn't imagine actually going through with getting a tattoo. She was such a baby about that kind of stuff.

Over by the impressive Christmas tree near the bay window, Jason and Marcus were talking. The boys. Smiling, Aria joined them and tucked her hand into Jason's pocket, enjoying his warmth and the smell of his cologne.

"Jason apparently is loving his new scarf," Marcus said. He'd transformed himself, Aria noticed. Gone was the surly guy in jeans and an attitude who'd been such a pain at the mall. Now he wore a fresh suit and tie, his hair was slicked back, and the sparkle was back in his blue eyes.

"Of course I love it," Jason said, kissing Aria's cheek.

"I think he'd be wearing it right now if it weren't hotter than hell in here," Marcus went on, grinning.

"Marcus just wishes he had a cashmere scarf of his own," Jason teased, taking Aria's hand. In his other hand, Jason held a glass of champagne, which he emptied with one gulp. From the look of his flushed cheeks, it wasn't his first.

Whatever, Aria thought. It was Christmas Eve. If Jason wanted to have fun, he should. She could always drive them home later. She put her half-empty cup of eggnog down on a nearby table without taking another sip.

Marcus reached over to punch Jason lightly on the shoulder. "Well, your girlfriend's got great taste, buddy."

"She sure does," Jason said. He indicated himself with a wave of his hand. "Hello. Exhibit A."

"Exhibit *Arrogant*, you mean," Aria teased him.

"You can't deny it," Jason said. He tugged on Aria's hand. "Come on. Let's get some more champagne!"

Later, after toasting the arrival of Christmas at midnight, as it started to snow outside, they danced in the living room. Aria thought there was nothing better than dancing on Christmas morning.

Unless, of course, your boyfriend was careening around like an idiot.

"Come on, Aria!" Jason brayed when a slow song came on. He grabbed her elbow, pulling her away from the conversation she'd been having with Emily's parents.

"Are you sure you don't want to sit down?" Aria asked. It seemed like Jason was a little too wound up for slow-dancing.

"I have to dance with my girl," he said. And his words would even have been sweet, too, if he hadn't slurred them, which kind of ruined the whole thing.

But a dance was a dance, Aria thought, and it was divine being nestled up close to her sweetie while slow music played and it snowed outside. It seemed like entire Christmas carols were dedicated to exactly that kind of feeling, so she closed her eyes and tried to imagine herself *inside* "I'll Be Home for Christmas," which had always been her favorite.

But Jason wouldn't let her drift away into happy, Christmasy space. He kept trying to throw some old-timey moves into the middle of things, like a dip or a twirl. The boy had clearly had too much champagne. Plus, Jason was a ham. Marcus was the talented performer, but it was Jason who craved the spotlight.

As Aria was trying to keep Jason under control, she happened to glance over at Marcus and Emily. They held each other close, swaying slightly to the music. There were no dramatic, silly twirls. They looked peaceful. Together. Complete.

Until Marcus looked up, and just for a moment, locked eyes with Aria.

It was like the room fell away. Like the rest of the world dissolved into nothing, leaving only Marcus's blue eyes.

Aria couldn't seem to catch a breath.

Then Jason stumbled across her toes again, bringing her back to herself.

"Sorry," Jason murmured, then dropped his face in Aria's neck.

Aria sighed. *I'll be home for Christmas*, the singer warbled plaintively, *if only in my dreams.*

When she looked across the room again, Marcus was gazing back down at Emily.

The way he should, of course.

Just like Aria should be looking at Jason.

She didn't look across the room again.

The day after Christmas, after too many cookies, too much cleaning up, and just enough family time, Aria pulled into the parking lot of Matthew's Diner. Matthew's was the favorite hangout of the foursome: her, Emily, Marcus, and Jason. This afternoon, though, it would be just the girls.

As she parked her mom's SUV, Aria thought about the millions of times, even before boys were in the picture, that she and Emily had compared notes and made sense of the world over cheese fries in one of Matthew's cracked red leather booths. The funny thing was that Matthew's kind of sucked, Aria reflected with a smile as she hurried across the frigid parking lot. Since this was New Jersey, land of a zillion diners, it was actually sort of difficult to find one with the rude service, mediocre food, and general dinginess of Matthew's. But none of that had ever mattered. It was just *their* diner.

Once Emily and Aria had both gotten boyfriends — miraculously, around the same time — the boys had joined them at Matthew's. The four of them had practically taken up residence in the corner booth with the broken tabletop jukebox. They'd never missed the music, though, not with Emily around to lead impromptu sing-alongs. Going to Matthew's with Marcus and Jason and texting Emily at Oberlin just hadn't been the same.

Aria skipped up the steps and went inside, not in the least surprised to discover that Emily wasn't there yet. It was Aria who was justly famous for always being on time — Emily, historically, would rush in ten minutes late to everything, rolling her green eyes, apologizing profusely, and promising to set her watch ten minutes ahead so that it would never happen again.

Smiling, Aria settled herself into their usual booth, ordered two Diet Cokes and the usual plate of goopy cheese fries, and waited. About fifteen minutes later, Emily pushed through the doors. She paused for a moment at the entrance, and Aria found herself looking at her closest friend in the world as if she were a stranger.

Emily was dressed differently, for one thing. Back in high school, she had been the typical J. Crew prep girl — pink cable-knit sweaters over collared shirts, straight-leg cords over pointy-toed boots. Aria had always been the more colorful dresser of the two, wearing funky head wraps, hoop earrings, and vintage baby-doll dresses over jeans. But now Emily wore battered and torn jeans, tall biker-girl boots, and a bright green 70s-style peacoat. She looked great, Aria thought, but she didn't really look like Emily. She looked kind of vintage-edgy. She looked like a college girl.

Which Aria reminded herself, was what Emily *was*. But it still made her stomach drop a little.

Just then, Emily looked up and spotted Aria. That same old, familiar, and infectious smile — the Cameron Diaz smile, Aria had nicknamed it — spread across her face. Immediately Aria relaxed.

Emily hurried over to the booth, and dropped into the bench across from Aria. "I'm *so* sorry," she said in a rush. "I saw your car was here, but I was on my cell phone with my friend Erin and she had this whole long, involved boy drama." Emily waved her hand in the air dismissively. "I can't even get into it." She pulled off her coat and set her cell phone on the table, which made Aria's breath catch. She and Emily had a hard-and-fast pact: no cell phones on the table. It was so rude, they always said. They'd both hated it when their other friends — particularly a girl named Missy Solomon, who they both found sort of irritating sometimes — did it.

"What?" Aria asked, tapping Emily's phone. "Have you jumped on the Missy Solomon bandwagon?"

Emily laughed. "God, Missy Solomon," she said. She shook her head. "I haven't thought about that girl in ages."

But she left her phone where it was.

And it didn't matter anyway, Aria thought, because everything else was fine. They picked at their cheese fries, and dunked them in ketchup. They giggled about how silly and drunk Emily's brother had been at the Christmas Eve party (not to mention Jason, Aria reminded Emily), and how they had both received the same annual gift certificate to The Gap from well-meaning relatives. Emily seemed more annoyed by that than Aria was, but Aria didn't mind playing along.

It was when they turned to the catching-up-on-their-lives part that things got a little weird.

"Come on," Aria said, leaning forward. "You always send me those short little e-mails claiming *so much drama* is happening, but that you can't write it all out so you'll tell me when we talk on the phone. But when we talk on the phone, we never seem to get around to it! You *promised* you'd tell me everything in person!"

"I know, I know," Emily moaned. "I wish I was better about keeping in touch — that was something I definitely didn't know about myself until I got to college."

Aria hadn't known it either. Before college, Emily had been

great about keeping in touch whenever she or Aria was away for any stretch of time, at summer camp and such. At least it was kind of good that Emily recognized it was her failure. Aria had been worried it might be hers.

"Now's your chance," Aria said, propping her elbows on the table. "I want to hear everything."

Emily shook her head, toying with a stray fry.

"I hardly know where to start," she said. She pursed her lips as if in thought. "Okay. Erin. The one I was just talking to?"

"I remember."

"Well, she lives on my hall," Emily said.

Then Emily launched into a long story about Erin, and a whole crew of other people who Aria couldn't seem to distinguish between. There were hall parties and dorm parties and drama over where to sit at dinner — which all sounded half-unreal to Aria, as if Emily was talking about some TV show Aria didn't watch.

So in the end, Emily just sort of sighed when Aria confessed that she was confused about the story of why Erin and all the other girls were mad at Sara, but couldn't tell her, because of some guy named Rob.

Or something.

"I guess you had to be there," Emily said. "It's kind of complicated if you don't know everybody."

Aria was determined not to get upset about that. It was just a story about people Aria didn't know and might not ever meet. She thought it might be better to talk about things she and Emily still had in common.

"Let me tell you about your boyfriend," Aria began with a grin. "I've never seen anyone miss someone as much as he misses you. And those girls who hang all over him would kill to help him ease his pain, *if* he gave any of them the time of day."

"Of course they would," Emily said, but she was fingering her cell phone. Either she wasn't worried about Marcus, or she'd forgotten exactly how skanky some of the girls they went to school with could be.

"Marcus and I set up Emily dates," Aria went on. "You know, we basically just hung around together and did Emily-type things. Like came here and had cheese fries. Or went ice-skating on the Duck Pond when the weather got cold. It was like an interactive way to miss you." As she spoke, Aria felt an odd twinge. It wasn't like she was telling a lie about her and Marcus's time together. Or was she?

"That's so sweet," Emily said distractedly when Aria stopped talking, but her attention was diverted by her phone ringing. She picked it up to check the caller ID, and Aria watched her face light up. But then she looked at Aria and put the phone back down without answering the call.

"My roommate," Emily said. "She's completely over her

family and can't believe she has to stay in her hometown for, like, six weeks. She's flipping out."

She said it as if she expected Aria to commiserate. Maybe Aria would have, but she loved their hometown. She was worried Emily might feel the same way as her roommate. When the phone rang a second time, Emily clucked her tongue.

"Oops," she said. "This is Carolyn. She's having major boyfriend trouble. Just let me make sure she's okay."

While she did that — right there at the table! The way she used to scorn! — Aria racked her brain, trying to figure out why Emily seemed so distant.

And then it hit her.

Duh.

What girl wanted to hear all about how her boyfriend had done all the things he used to do with her, but with another girl?

Emily probably hated the fact that Aria got to spend all that time with Marcus when she barely got to see him anymore. Aria could have kicked herself. How could she be so insensitive?

I'll apologize she thought then, *and make it clear that while Marcus and I are closer than when Emily was around, we're just friends who bonded over missing the same important person.*

That was bound to make everything all right.

Just as soon as Emily got off the phone.

✳   ✳   ✳

By the afternoon of New Year's Eve, Aria decided she felt much better about everything. Not that she had been feeling *bad* about anything, necessarily, she thought as she waited for the heat in the car to kick in. She shivered and turned the dial all the way up into the red zone.

Driving over to Emily's house gave her the time and space to think about all the stuff that had been going on since Christmas. Which was a whole lot of nothing. Aria had visited her grandparents and Jason's parents, and had gone to the movies with Marcus, Emily, and Jason one night. The double date had been fun, almost like a time warp. Emily and Aria had sat in the middle of the two boys so they could whisper whenever they liked. Then, afterward, it had been back to Matthew's for ham, egg, and cheese sandwiches. And cheese fries, of course. It was like old times in every way, except . . .

Emily seemed so, well, *aloof* every time the subject of Marcus came up. And Aria hadn't even been in touch with Marcus lately, wanting him and Emily to have their alone time.

Frowning, Aria put in the earpiece of her cell and hit speed dial.

"Do you think Emily might be weirded out that Marcus and I are friends?" she asked Jason the moment he answered his cell phone.

"What?" Jason's voice sounded muffled. "No. Why would she care?"

It didn't sound much like *he* cared, Aria thought.

"She's just, I don't know . . . she's just all *different*," Aria began haltingly. And she makes all these calls and is always texting her *other* friends in the middle of conversations —"

"You guys seemed cool at the movie," Jason interrupted her. Now he definitely sounded impatient.

"What are you doing?" Aria asked, turning onto Emily's street.

"I'm about to head into the locker room," Jason replied, with a snap in his voice. "I thought you were calling to wish me luck."

Aria hadn't *exactly* forgotten about the big game, since she was on her way to pick up Marcus and Emily so they could all cheer on Jason from the stands. But she hadn't really been thinking about what Jason might be doing to prepare for it, either. "I *was* about to wish you luck," she lied.

"Listen," Jason said, and she could tell he didn't believe her. "It's probably weird for Emily. She's the one who doesn't belong anymore. That's got to suck."

"You're probably right," Aria agreed, although she wasn't at all sure. Emily didn't seem particularly weirded out. She seemed relieved when her college life intruded on her old life.

"Of course I'm right," Jason said. "Now, I have to concentrate on the important stuff — wining this game. Unless you want me to lose for some reason."

Aria sighed, assured Jason that she wanted him to win, and clicked off. Sometimes it was hard to believe that she'd been dating Jason for almost a year and a half. That was long enough, she thought, for him to know that she supported him, even if she was worried about something else.

Not that it mattered, Aria decided as she parked outside Emily's house. Weirdness be damned! It was New Year's Eve, there was the big football game, and then a huge party at one of the player's houses that night. Since half the town was going and Aria was a senior, her parents didn't expect her home until two A.M., which was way later than her usual curfew. A shiver of anticipation ran through her at the thought.

She opened Emily's back door and let herself in, the way she had since the seventh grade.

But in the next instant, she wished she'd rung the doorbell.

Marcus and Emily stood in the family room. Emily had her arms crossed over her chest, and Marcus's face was tight with tension. The room was way too quiet.

It didn't take a genius to figure out that Aria had walked into a serious fight.

"Hey, guys!" she said brightly, feigning ignorance. "Happy New Year!"

"I guess it's just you and me for the game," Marcus said without looking at Emily, who was not, Aria noticed, wearing her Christmas necklace.

"You're kidding," Aria said, searching Emily's face. "You know Jason wants all of us there!"

Emily shrugged. "You remember my friend Carolyn?" she said. "She's a total mess and I have to go see her. I'll be back for the party tonight, though. Aria, do you think Jason will hate me if I miss the game?"

"Yes," Marcus said, shaking his head at her. "Since this is his last New Year's Eve game for his entire high school career."

Aria cleared her throat, not wanting to make Emily feel worse. "I guess Carolyn needs you."

"I knew you'd understand," Emily said, rushing over to hug Aria. She turned back to look at Marcus.

"I don't really understand why some girl you've known for a couple of months is more important than the friends you've had your whole life," Marcus said to Emily in a low, bitter tone that Aria had never heard from him before. "But what do I know?"

Aria wanted to agree with him. *Choose us!* she wanted to yell at Emily, but she was too afraid that Emily had already chosen. And she couldn't deal with what that meant. She couldn't even let herself think about it.

"Come on, Marcus," Aria said instead, forcing a smile. "We have a football game to cheer."

Up in the stands, Aria clapped along with the crowd, but her thoughts were elsewhere.

Down on the field, a helmeted Jason was running around, fighting hard against the neighboring town's team. Aria knew Jason assumed she watched him every single second he was on the field, and sure, she tried. But Jason didn't know how much fun it was to be one of the crowd, up in the students' section. Not to mention that it could be difficult to pick between the identically dressed players. Aria knew better than to explain this to her boyfriend. If he wanted to believe that she knew exactly where he was at every moment he played, well, he should go on thinking that.

"Hey." Marcus's voice came from behind her. "Earth to Aria. You okay?"

"I . . ." she started to say, but stopped — brought up short by the intense look on Marcus's face.

Everything around them seemed to be at a sudden distance.

Aria didn't know what was going on, but her knees felt elastic.

"Aria . . ." Marcus said her name in a whisper. As if he'd been waiting a long time to say it exactly like that.

No, no, no, Aria thought.

"Did you see that last play?" she asked desperately.

"I've been trying so hard," Marcus said slowly, at first. Then he met Aria's gaze and kept on talking. Faster. "I thought, you know, that we were just friends, and that I was missing Emily."

"Both of those things are true!" Her voice came out strange and thin in the air.

"Yeah, and for a long time that was all it was," Marcus said. "Something changed, Aria. *We* changed. I knew even before I saw Emily on Christmas Eve, but seeing her . . ." He shook his head. "I think I'm —"

"Crazy?" Aria supplied angrily, before he could finish. "I can't believe you're saying these things! Emily loves you. She *trusts* you!"

"Forget about Emily for a minute," Marcus said, frowning.

"Yeah, you know what? I can't do that," Aria snapped at him. "She's my best friend!"

"Is she?" Marcus replied. "Because I thought your best friend was, well, me. I mean, hasn't it been strange with her home? Haven't you picked up the phone, like, a thousand times to call me but stopped, because suddenly the fact that we usually talk that much seems, I don't know, bad? Like we shouldn't *want* to talk to each other that much?"

"No!" Aria exclaimed, but inside she felt dizzy. How could this be *happening*?

"I don't think we're just friends," Marcus continued, practically whispering. "I think it's something else, and I think you feel it, too."

Aria discovered that she wasn't holding her breath anymore. Now she'd gone the other way, and was breathing heavily. Panting, practically, as if she'd just gone for a run.

This wasn't real.

It was *too* real.

"What about Jason?" she finally managed to ask. "He's down there on the field, supposedly one of your best friends, and this is what you're doing while he's playing his heart out? What kind of friend are you?"

"A shitty one," Marcus replied, shrugging a little bit. "Which is something I'll have to deal with. But, Aria, come on. You can't tell me you don't feel the same." But there was a tremor of doubt in his voice that revealed how vulnerable he was feeling.

It all made sense, Aria thought in some distant part of her brain — the part that was still capable of thought. The rest of her was frozen in shock, but there was still that tiny piece of her whispering the truth she didn't want to face.

It all made sense.

No wonder she was so worried that Emily might suspect there was something less-than-innocent about Aria's relationship with Marcus. And no wonder Marcus had been so indifferent at the mall that day they went shopping. He hadn't wanted to deal with the fact that Emily was coming home. He'd wanted to continue uninterruped with what was growing between him and Aria.

Aria knew it was true.

And she also knew that admitting it would mean betraying her best friend in the most awful way possible. Especially if

Emily might have already picked up on what was happening between her boyfriend and her best friend.

So it had to stop right there.

It had to end.

"You feel the same way," Marcus said again, more urgently this time. "I know it."

He reached over and touched Aria's cheek so gently, so sweetly that she ached even as she jerked her head away.

"I don't feel the same," she told him in a very clear, very firm tone. "I'm just wondering how I'm going to explain this conversation to Emily."

They stood there staring at each other for another long moment. All around them, people cheered, and the band played wild, infectious beats that should have had them dancing. Any other day, they would have been. Aria could remember other games, other years. She and Emily and Marcus cheering, the three of them dancing like idiots, happy to be supporting Jason. That was the way things were *supposed* to be. This was all wrong.

"My mistake," Marcus said finally, and something dark moved into his eyes. Aria felt like the same thing crept over her, but she looked away.

"A big mistake," she whispered.

"I'm out of here," Marcus choked out, like it was hard to speak. He sounded . . . *heartbroken*. The word sprang into Aria's head before she could stop it.

But Marcus was already moving away from her, making his way down the bleachers. Soon enough, he was swallowed up in the crowd and gone.

Something that felt like a sob rolled up from deep inside Aria then, but she refused to let it take her over.

She would not cry.

She was a good friend. She was a good girlfriend.

The crowd erupted all around her, and Aria blinked, dazed. It took her a moment to realize that the home team had scored.

Not just her home team — her boyfriend.

Jason was doing his trademark celebratory dance in the end zone. She could recognize that wiggle of his, even from so far away, and then the announcer's voice boomed out his name, confirming it.

When she saw he was looking up at her, flushed and victorious, Aria waved and smiled. From so far away, she'd bet the smile looked real.

The football player throwing the New Year's Eve party was named Brett. His parents lived way out on the outskirts of town, and had an old red barn at the far end of their property, which they let Brett use to stage his ridiculous, life-altering parties a couple times a year. Brett's barn had been converted into a giant rec room. There was a huge flat-screen television, a pool table, and about sixteen ways for kids to get into trouble.

Brett was the closest thing kids in Aria's town had to Neptune High's 09ers in *Veronica Mars*.

Aria and Jason made their way across the frozen field toward the barn. Even from a distance, she could hear the music pounding and the sounds of people going wild. At Brett's place, anything could happen, and it usually did before midnight.

Aria shivered slightly in her puffy jacket, and Jason looked over at her. It was already late — almost eleven o'clock — because of the impromptu celebratory dinner Jason's parents had thrown in honor of his game-winning touchdown. Not that Aria begrudged him a great ending to his high school football career. Of course she didn't. She was totally and completely supportive.

"Something wrong?" Jason asked.

"Nope." She smiled at him, smoothing away the slight frown she hadn't realized she was wearing. "It's just cold out here."

"You'll warm up when we get inside," Jason assured her. He looked as if he was about to say something else, but ducked his head instead.

She felt a surge of relief when they walked inside the barn. It seemed as if every kid Aria had ever met wanted to celebrate Jason. As soon as he appeared, there were cheers and toasts, and the louder of his linebacker pals surged around him, chanting his name. They even picked him up at one point, which was Aria's cue to back away.

"You're soooo lucky!" a girl Aria had never seen before trilled at her, appearing at Aria's side. "Jason is a *hero!*"

The girl had so many stars in her eyes, Aria was surprised she could see.

Jason's feet were allowed to hit the floor again, finally. Then the winning touchdown was described. And reenacted. And described again, to a chorus of chants and cheers.

Not wanting to drag him away from his fans — and not wanting to hear about the same play one more time — Aria slipped away during another reenactment. There were enough gaga girls around, she reasoned. She wouldn't be missed.

Everyone else looked like they were having a blast. Kids from her high school waved at Aria as she wandered by, but she didn't stop to talk.

Out behind the barn, there was a bonfire going in the fire pit, and Aria drifted toward the flames. She thought it would be nice to warm herself, and maybe gaze into the dancing fire for a while. She could spend hours staring into the fireplace at her parents' house. The colors and shapes seemed to ease her troubles, or hypnotize her into forgetting about them, or something.

But somehow she wasn't surprised when she found a place on the nearest log, and looked up to see that there was someone already sitting there.

Marcus.

As if she was drawn to him even when she wasn't looking for him.

She let out a small sigh.

They looked at each other for a moment.

"I'm sorry —" Aria began.

"I shouldn't have —" Marcus said at the same time.

Embarrassed, Aria looked down. She felt so awkward around him, suddenly, and it was the craziest thing, because until that afternoon she'd practically reveled in how easy and laid-back their relationship was.

"I know I put you in a terrible position at the game today," Marcus said. "What were you supposed to say? I'm really sorry."

"So you . . ." Aria shook her head, not sure what she was asking. "I was thinking that you and Emily had a fight before I showed up, so was that why . . . ?"

Marcus stopped facing the warmth of the fire, turning to look at Aria instead. She was sure she could feel ten times the heat coming from him.

"I said I was sorry for throwing that on you like that," he said, watching her face. "I didn't say I was sorry for what I said."

Aria felt her mouth move, but she couldn't seem to say anything. Or look away.

"I can't stop thinking about you," he told her. "I don't

know when it happened. One minute it was all about missing Emily and then — it was just about you."

"But . . ." Aria still couldn't seem to do anything except stare at him.

"I'm breaking up with Emily," Marcus said. He sounded upset, but also matter-of-fact. His eyes were still intent on Aria's. "If you don't feel the way I do, that's cool. But I can't . . ." He shook his head. "I'm not going to pretend that things are the way they used to be, because *we* aren't the way we used to be."

His face softened then, and he reached out to her again.

"Marcus . . ." She tried to speak, to say the huge things that were blocking her chest and making it so hard to breathe.

"Don't cry," Marcus whispered. "Please don't cry. I can't stand it."

Which was when Aria realized there were tears rolling down her face.

And that they were almost entirely alone at the fire, because everyone else was headed inside.

The New Year was practically upon them.

"I do feel it," Aria told him. She wiped her eyes. "I feel what you feel. Of course I do."

"I hoped you might." He was looking at her as if he wanted to drink her in.

Aria couldn't seem to stop crying. And then the words

began to pour out of her — all the words she'd been afraid to say before.

"I just don't know what to do about Emily," she said through a broken sob. "Or Jason. They're our best friends! How can we do this to them? I don't want to hurt anyone, Marcus, not even if it means I get to be with you —"

"Aria." He smoothed his hand over her braids, and tugged on the end of one. "People grow apart. That's what happens. Isn't it?"

"I don't know," Aria whispered. "I don't know anything."

And then everything seemed to slow down. Small, perfect snowflakes began to flutter down from the deep black sky up above. Aria noticed how close together she and Marcus were sitting. She could feel his heartbeat as she leaned into the crook of his neck. It seemed like a dream — a dream she'd been having for a long time, but had refused to think about upon waking.

Until now.

She tilted her head back and let herself gaze into those wonderful blue eyes of his.

And then he kissed her.

She expected Christmas magic.

Instead, she got New Year's fire.

Marcus kissed her the way Aria had always dreamed of being kissed. His lips were soft but urgent. The kiss was hot and addictive and so good she wanted to cheer from pure joy.

It was amazing, and Aria never wanted it to end.

When he pulled away, they were both smiling wide, giddy smiles. Inside the barn, Aria could hear wild cheering, and she guessed that meant the clock had chimed midnight. Maybe just as they were kissing.

It was perfect.

Until Aria noticed the other figure standing there near the fire, watching the two of them intently.

Emily.

For a moment, no one moved.

They all just stared at one another, as if rooted to the frozen ground beneath their feet.

"Oh, my God," Aria whispered, horrified, when she could finally speak. "Oh, my God, *Emily!*"

Aria scrambled backward, away from Marcus, who wasn't moving. In fact, Aria calmed down enough to see that he and Emily were just looking at each other, almost as if they'd never seen each other before.

"Emily," Aria began. She had no idea what was going to come out of her mouth next. "This is so . . . I mean, I would *never* . . . I don't know *how* . . ."

"This is my fault," Marcus said, but Aria barely heard him. She could only look at Emily.

"I have to say," Emily said, her voice brittle, "this is not how I envisioned my New Year's."

Emily still didn't look at Aria. She was watching Marcus with an odd expression on her face. The expression was odd because it didn't seem appalled or angry or crushed. It looked as if Emily was puzzling something out.

Aria didn't know what to do.

She stood there, aware of the chill in the air and the crackle of the flames, and stared at Emily, studying her delicate face, her strawberry-blonde hair. It was like she was cataloging her best friend, imprinting her, in case this was the last time they ever spoke.

She couldn't believe she was even thinking such a thing, but how else could this end? Aria had committed the ultimate betrayal. It was unforgivable.

"Marcus," Emily said finally, her tone softer, "can I talk to Aria for a minute? Alone?"

Marcus nodded once, sent Aria a single meaningful look, and then headed for the barn, leaving Aria to face what she'd done.

"Oh, Emily," she whispered into the dark, snow-sprinkled night. She was afraid to look at her friend. "I don't know how this happened. I don't know how to fix it."

"You always misread people, Aria," Emily said, and her voice wasn't bitter, or furious, or any of the things Aria thought it should have been. Something in Emily's voice made Aria feel like it was okay to start talking. Maybe if she was finally honest with her friend, she'd make sense of things.

So she explained about how close she and Marcus had become, how she'd realized she didn't feel half as close to Jason.

"I didn't mean for this . . ." Aria sighed. "I didn't even know it was happening. I just wanted everything to be the way it used to be."

"So you thought you should hook up with my boyfriend?" Emily snorted. "Great plan."

Aria squared her shoulders and pushed on. "You've been so different since you went away," she explained. "It was like you couldn't wait to escape! Like you hated everything here. Maybe even me." It was so hard to say that last part. She hadn't even known how scared she was of putting it out there, where Emily might confirm it.

"I could never hate you, Aria," Emily whispered. She waved her hand over the fire, and over Aria. "But maybe I don't know you as well as I used to."

"I'm *exactly* the same!" Aria cried.

"That's not true, is it?" Emily asked softly. "You just don't want to admit that you've changed. But we both have." Emily sighed, and stuck her hands in her jeans pockets.

"Carolyn didn't have any emergency today," she said.

Aria blinked, not really following that change in subject.

"Okay," she said.

"I was the one having the emergency," Emily confessed. "Because everything's so different, Aria. I thought things would be the same no matter how far away I was, but it isn't true. I love you, and I love Marcus, too, but . . ." She broke off and hugged herself around the waist. "I was going to break things off with him before you came over today. I don't know how to say this without being mean, but I've moved on."

"I think I understand, Em, " Aria managed to say.

"I have this whole new life," Emily went on, her expression intense. "And I didn't know how to start telling you about it, because all you want to talk about is this life here."

"This is the only one I know!" Aria cried, stung. "And it's the only one we shared!"

"I would have talked to you about all of this — like how far apart Marcus and I had drifted, some of the guys I've met at school, all those things, but it seemed like you and he were so close. I didn't want you to be mad at me."

"I thought *you* were mad at *me*," Aria whispered.

"You're my best friend," Emily said. She looked down for a moment, then back at Aria. "This thing with you and Marcus is a little bizarre, but also kind of makes sense, I think."

Aria found she was crying again.

"I'm so sorry," Aria whispered. "I had no idea I was the kind of person who could do this."

"Neither did I," Emily admitted, and then after a moment, that wicked smile of hers spread across her face. "I think it's about time you let yourself be more than just *good*, Aria."

"There's nothing *wrong* with being good," Aria protested.

"No, but being a little bad is so much more fun," Emily said, laughing, and despite herself, Aria giggled, but it turned into a hiccup. "Or, in your case, being slightly less good."

"Oh, Em," Aria said, closing the distance between them. "I don't want to lose you."

"You won't. You can't," Emily said fiercely, came forward, and swept Aria into a hug.

Not as if nothing had happened, but as if everything had. And they were both okay, and together.

Aria knew exactly where to find him, because it's where she would have gone: Matthew's.

He looked up from the booth in the corner when she walked in, and watched her as she made her way to him.

"I'm going to take this as a good sign," he said when she sat down across from him.

"You're drinking cider," Aria said, nodding to the mug in his hand and inhaling the sweet tang. Christmas Eve at the mall came back to her in a rush — back when they were still pretending.

"I don't know," he said, but he was smiling. "I just had a craving."

Aria reached across the tabletop and took his hand between hers, marveling at the simple act of it. Touching Marcus. Tracing the shape of his fingers and his palm. Now that he'd opened her eyes to what was really happening between them,

Aria felt like she could hardly wait to discover all the things she hadn't allowed herself even to wish for.

"I don't know how I didn't know this was happening," she whispered.

Marcus smiled, his blue eyes warm on her face.

"Well," he said, "it was complicated."

Aria let her head drop, but she didn't let go of Marcus's hand.

"I have to tell Jason," she said. "I just kind of ran out of the party and asked Emily to tell him I wasn't feeling well. I had to find you."

Marcus obviously liked the sound of that, because he flipped their hands around so he could do the holding and the tracing. He moved his fingers across Aria's palm.

"I could tell him," he offered. "If you want."

That would be like my buying Emily a Christmas present from you, Aria thought with a smile. In other words, ridiculous. It would be painful, and Jason was going to be hurt, but Aria knew she had to do it herself. She owed Jason that much. She owed Marcus that, too. He'd been so honest — he'd taken all the risks. Now it was her turn.

"I'll tell him," she said. "I'll do it tonight. And then, tomorrow . . ."

"Tomorrow will be all for us," Marcus agreed, still smiling that wide, pleased smile.

Aria felt a wave of emotion swell inside her, and almost

had to close her eyes. It suddenly really did feel like a new year. A new start.

Aria reached over and picked up the cinnamon shaker from the wire display, and shook it over Marcus's cider.

"There," she said. "The perfect amount."

"Finally," Marcus said, and then he leaned over and kissed her. His lips were sweet, with that special, delicious kick that was all Marcus.

And just like that, Aria knew everything would be, if not perfect, then at least pretty darn close.

✳ ✳ ✳ ✳ ✳ ✳ ✳

SCENES FROM
A CINEMATIC
NEW YEAR'S

✳

By Nina Malkin

✳ ✳ ✳ ✳ ✳ ✳ ✳

Scene I: FAUX SNOW

Go ahead, pinch yourself. Rub your eyes. Shake your head. Could it really be him? Right here among the masses, Connor Moline — known to millions as Danny Stiles on *Pinot's Point*? Believe it. This is one juicy star sighting. Not that he's here by choice — no way, bay-bee. Checking out the bogus blizzard is Tommy's idea, and Tommy's a hammerhead when he gets an idea, keeps battering on about it till Connor gives in. Connor's magnanimous that way. His boy Tommy, what a pisser, and totally loyal — but not the brightest bulb in the marquee. He's like a little kid, Tommy is. This time, it's the snow; Tommy just *has* to see the snow.

"Come on, dude, come on! Snow! Dude! Come on! Snow!" That's Tommy.

Throughout the holiday season, in the middle of LA's finest al fresco mall, there's a snowstorm — two, in fact: the seven P.M. snowing and the nine P.M. snowing. Machines crank out mass quantities of perfect, fluffy, six-pointed flakes while onlookers *ooh* and *ah*. Where else but Hollywood, huh? Personally, Connor doesn't get it. What's a white Christmas compared to a sunny SoCal golden one? Besides, they're all going up to Tahoe for New Year's — Connor, Tommy, the rest of the crew, and a bevy of fine ladies — they'll be catching air in fresh powder, the real deal, so what up with a cheesy tourist attraction.

"Dude, come on, it'll be fun!" Tommy pleads.

"What are you, in kindergarten?" Connor's only half-annoyed — how mad can you get at a nineteen-year-old who may still believe in Santa? "It's faux snow, you moron. . . ."

"You have to admit it has a certain meta-ironic appeal." This is from Morgan. Stubble-faced fortune hunter, keyboard player in Jared Padalecki's neo-New Wave band, the antithesis of Tommy in the smarts department. So if Morgan thinks it's cool . . . "Be a sport, Con-Man," Morgan adds. "The snow must go on, and we must observe it. It's an anthropological phenomenon."

Okay, all right, Connor's convinced. Of course they do some preliminary hits off the vaporizer to get in the mood. Of course Connor's trademark sunlit curls are now hidden under a baseball cap, the inscrutable gray-green eyes that gaze weekly from TV screens across America obscured behind wraparound shades. Of course they're standing in the VIP area, enjoying complimentary Glo-Balls (basically, Vanilla Stoli snow cones). But apparently anyone can get into a VIP area — anyone with a rack, at least — so just as Connor could've predicted, as soon as the phony meteorology event begins, he's sighted. First it's a pair of twins, straight out of Podunk. A double shot of freckled redheads in cutoffs and Disneyland

T-shirts, skin pink from too much sun and not enough SPF. There's the requisite whispering behind their hands to make sure this is really happening, and pulling compact mirrors out of counterfeit Fendis to compose themselves.

Now, here it comes. The onslaught . . .

"Omigod! Hi!"

"Hi! Omigod!"

"It's you, omigod, isn't it? Danny! I mean Connor! Omigod, Connor Mol*eeene*!?"

That does it — that high-decibel, fan-frequency squeal alerts all other females in the vicinity. Not just the usual suspects, either. Little girls, like nine. Desperate house-wives — geez, desperate grandmas. Fortunately, Connor knows the drill: "Hey, you got me, thank you, that's sweet, thanks a lot. . . ." He smiles. They melt. A few are compelled to touch him, fluttery, bird-wing brushes; no one cops an overt feel. He signs stuff — a shopping bag from Neiman's, an invite to a dance club, the rounded swell of a bold girl's breast. Oh, damn, now they're taking out camera phones. Give 'em an inch . . .

Connor shoots Morgan a scowl, like "What I tell you, man!" Morgan puts his palms up — "Not my fault you're a chick magnet!" — but punches Chess, and Chess punches Jay, so now they're all aware that a hasty retreat is imminent. Well, not all. Tommy's oblivious; Tommy's catching newly manufactured snowflakes on his tongue.

The whole surreal routine lasts four minutes, five max — that's all Connor can handle. Then he flicks the vibe to "off." He is dunzo. It's subtle, but even the most obsessive fan can pick up on it, that her dream has come true and now it's time to be appreciative . . . and be out.

Look, a guy's gotta do what a guy's gotta do. Connor's never been outright mean to a fan — well, there was that time in that club when that girl was really drunk. He needed all his wingmen to pry her off his belt buckle, but the barnacle babe no doubt still hasn't washed her hands after laying them on Connor Moline.

Now, he and the boys bolt for the exit with the singlemindedness of a SWAT team in a Bruckheimer blockbuster and pile into Connor's Escalade — he calls it the Tank, his everyday run-around vehicle. Next stop, Rob Zombie's reindeer barbecue in Beechwood Canyon. Laughing, relieved — another narrow escape! — the star and his inner circle fade into a landscape lush with palm trees and bougainvillea. No chance of snow.

Scene II: FANTASY ISLAND

A long, lithe girl in a king-sized bed, Lisle Blunke lies indolently between a set of sheets — Egyptian cotton and Thai silk, the thread count so high and the weave so tight they could stop a bullet. Lisle has nothing else to do all day but roll around in lingerie, indulging fantasies. Easy, since Lisle's fantasy is cut and pasted to her reality. She tosses to the left, tawny limbs contrasting against the expanse of ivory fabric. She turns right, and the small smile on her lips reveals not *precisely* what flickers behind her shadowed eyelids but certainly a hint that Lisle's slo-mo, soft-focus mind movie would garner an NC-17.

This unfurling fantasy costars a boy with enigmatic eyes and messy surfer hair, demanding hands, and a teasing tongue — the boy she inwardly calls Danny Connor. Naturally, Lisle knows the difference between Connor Moline and Danny Stiles. In reality, Lisle is going out with Connor, has been for two months. In fantasy, however — in moments like this, every inch of flesh a celebration of blissful indolence — Lisle fixates on Danny. That is her secret. She's *with* Connor, but she *prefers* Danny.

When Lisle first alit in Los Angeles, *Pinot's Point* was in its debut season — and although her English was nonexistent, on some visceral level Lisle understood the twisted family drama with the sardonic edge. The *feel* of the show — bright saturated colors, dizzying camera angles, the protracted pace of the dialogue — grabs people at a primal place in the psyche. It's decadent — and absolutely addictive, from slinky theme song to closing credits. So, along with countless anonymous viewers nationwide, Lisle was shocked and amazed by the unlikely metamorphosis of Danny Stiles.

For two years, Danny — youngest son of the eccentric Napa

Valley winery clan in the show — had been this little . . . what is the slang? Deek? Nerb? Dweeb, yes that's it. Cast for his squeaky voice and unruly mop, his too-long arms and sunken chest, Connor Moline *was* Danny Stiles. Then, seemingly overnight, Connor came into his own. He filled out — not just in terms of pecs and lats but in the face, so what had been hollow and drawn was now chiseled and proud — into the yummiest specimen of young manhood the viewing public would ever idolize. Naturally the creators of *Pinot's Point* couldn't continue to use him as comic relief; they capitalized on the newfound hot factor, spinning plot lines around Danny. And in ten easy episodes, Connor Moline catapulted smoothly and firmly into the stratosphere.

Everyone loves the new Danny; Lisle just happens to be the one dating him — oops, not *Danny . . . Connor.* All she had to do was place herself in his line of vision one night at Blake 33; Connor feigned blasé but almost dropped his miniburger at the sight of Belgian megababe Lisle Blunke, her sumptuous proportions displayed in a Dolce minidress and open-toed Manolos. A tactical maneuver on Lisle's part; she's ready to segue from supermodel to actress, and hooking up with the hottest male star in television is an E! ticket to the next level. The paparazzi simply adore them, such a gorgeous couple — so tall, so tan, so sculpted, so blond. Come Friday, when Lisle joins Connor in Tahoe for New Year's Eve, she'll be snowboarding by day and snuggling by night with every girl's desire. And if in the process she impresses the players Connor has invited along, cool. Lisle knows how to multitask.

Now, however, she must concentrate on the matter at hand. This bed, these pillows, a soundstage in New York — where she's been all week.

"Beautiful, Lisle, beautiful!" whisper-shouts the director, hovering on a scaffold above her. "Yes, yes! Like that! Soooo sexy!"

Lisle strokes herself across the sheet from left shoulder to right hip with a small contented purr. Yes, she is very pleased with the way things are progressing. Except for one teensy item. If only Connor were more like his character. On the show, Danny Stiles is one of those delicious guys who haven't got a clue how delicious they are. Off the set, however, Connor Moline behaves like he was born the heir apparent to Brad Pitt. He swaggers and slouches, his laugh can be like the bark of a Doberman, and — sin of sins! — he can be rude to waiters. Everyone in Hollywood knows courtesy to service people is de rigeur, since service people are a direct line to the tabloids. But Connor Moline doesn't care. In real life, he doesn't follow anyone's script but his own.

Scene III: OCEAN VIEW

If there's one thing that bugs Connor Moline, it's how chicks always stand on ceremony. All day long he's memorizing lines, hitting his marks — is it a crime to want things looser in his personal life? Connor's sister, Olivia, is the worst like that. What a little tight-ass — and she's only thirteen. It was nag, nag, nag, trying to get Connor to spend Christmas Day with her and their dad, and he intended to, but something came up. As in Rayne, Lisle's housemate. Not that Connor was cheating. He and Lisle, they're by no means exclusive — that would be bad for his image, and she's fully in the loop on that. But Lisle, her ego's so fragile she'd disintegrate if she knew he spent Christmas discovering that Rayne is both naughty and nice. Hey, Lisle's loss — accepting the last-minute booking in NYC was *her* decision.

Idly Connor wonders how much flesh Lisle will flaunt in the commercial. Again, her decision, but if she hopes to be taken seriously as an actor, she's got to watch the smut quotient. Like Connor, he's not one of those dime-a-dozen TV bimboys always taking his shirt off. It's all carefully worded in his contract — he's paid extra for every button undone, every bit of phony sweat they mist on him. That swimming scene in the season premiere with guest star Taryn Manning? It paid for his '63 GTO.

That Bitch — capital B. Not Taryn, no, no, no — she's a real sweetheart. The Bitch is his favorite new toy, one lean, mean head-games machine; looks cool, runs hot and cold. He loves that car — cherry red, white interior, blistering 389 engine could take you to Mars and back during a commercial break . . . *if* she's in the mood.

Ha! Thinking of difficult females brings Connor back to Olivia. So he wasn't nestled in the bosom of his splintered family on the actual date of December 25. The Molines were never much on church, until Mrs. Moline took this self-help seminar that turned out to be a front for a cult. She joined in '03, and it made Connor recoil even further from anything remotely affiliated with religion — traditional, alternative, whatever.

Besides, it's not like he didn't get Olivia a ton of presents. He dispatched a personal shopper to Fred Segal Melrose with a blank check, then had the gifts messengered to the Moline homestead in Reseda. Maybe he should cut the kid some slack, though. She's been basically raising herself since age nine. That's when their parents officially split, and their mom became a proper member of the Ministry of Morris. And their dad receded into second adolescence. The chicks his dad dates? Let's just say Connor's convinced they go out with the old guy to get closer to him. And of course Connor's maxed out with *Pinot's*, so there's not much time for surrogate parenting — especially now that he bought his own place, the killer condo with a balcony practically touching the ocean.

Could be why Olivia's on clench about the Christmas ritual. Well, better face the music. First he grabs a loganberry juice from the fridge. Then he slips on a fresh T-shirt. Connor has developed a T-shirt problem; he can't wear the same one twice. Heading out to his terrace, he internally mocks himself with studied sarcasm and wonders if there's a Twelve-Step program for that. He takes a seat and gazes out, feeling, with no false modesty, like the king of all he surveys — Santa Monica pier to his left, the road to Malibu on his right, the entire Pacific stretching out in front of him, a giant salad of exotic blue lettuce. He flips his phone and punches in the number. He never did get around to putting it on speed dial.

Scene IV: SUBURBIA

Outside the house, it is seventy-two degrees; the lawn is green and each individual drop of sprinkler spray shines like a diamond in the sun. Within the house, it is sixty-eight degrees and spotless, clinically spotless, in the wake of a zealous cleaning woman. The house is empty, devoid of life, except for Olivia Moline, who sits in her sweats reading the liner notes of her new Abominant CD. When Connor's name appears on the caller ID, she carries the phone to the aluminum Christmas tree no one bothered to decorate.

"Yo, Liv-a-Snap!" Connor shouts with forced merriment.

"Oh," Olivia says. "It's you." Deliberately, she presses a fake silver pine needle into the meaty part of her palm. Some people choose to numb their pain; Olivia wants to feel hers to the fullest extent.

"You get the stuff — my presents?" Connor asks.

"Yes," she says. "They came." *Keep it to monosyllables,* she tells herself. *Talk too much and you'll betray emotion.*

"And . . . ?"

"And what?"

"A thank-you maybe." Connor tries to keep his tone genial. Olivia's just entering her awkward stage; if it's anything like his, it'll have a life expectancy of five years. Plus, her awkward stage is coinciding with her conscientious rejecter stage — Olivia's anti-fashion, anti-makeup, anti–blow-dryer, anti-zit cream; basically anti-anything, Connor concludes, that would make her existence somewhat less of a hell on earth.

"Gee, thanks, Connor," Olivia intones, but despite her deadpan she can't control the flood. "Thank you for validating conspicuous consumption. Thank you for exploiting third world countries where these trinkets were assembled under sweat-shop conditions. Thank you for pillaging trees with unrecycled gift wrap, and thank you for wasting fossil fuels on a messenger service."

Oh, she's good. She's real good. "Liv, don't be a classic bitch, okay?"

Olivia bites her lip, steels it into a sneer. Not that he can see it. Not that he would give a damn. "You stop being an asshole, I'll quit being a bitch. Deal?"

"What, you're pissed because I couldn't make it Christmas Day?" As if he didn't know. "Look, Olivia, I know you wanted me there, I know you wanted the whole Christmas hoo-hah, but something crucial came up. And . . . look, I'm sorry, okay?"

"Okay? No, Connor, not okay. But don't apologize, because *I'm* the one who's sorry. I'm sorry you thought you could buy me off with your bag full of overpriced presents, which for your information I have no intention of opening. They're going straight to a homeless shelter and I hope they bring someone happiness. Because the only person who could bring me happiness is lost to me. Lost . . ."

With a final click of the cordless, Olivia terminates the conversation. It's a quiet click, not the satisfying slam-down of those old-style phones, yet still an audible counterpart to disappointment, her only company in the otherwise empty house.

Scene V: THIS, THAT, AND THE OTHER THING

What a joke. Unbelievable, really. What the hell is he doing — in a car, on the road, by him*self* . . . him, Connor Moline?! When his crew, his girl, and a selection of soon-to-be associates, including the son of the CEO of Columbia Pictures, have already landed in Tahoe. A pitfall of his lofty position.

It starts at the crack of dawn, with Connor's publicist texting and calling every thirty seconds. The woman's a neurotic Chihuahua, a paramount pain in the ass, but that's what he pays her for. "'Sup, Anjolie?" Connor yawn-groans the greeting.

"Connor, you've *got* to do *AE* — it's the 'Star Chat' segment, you know how madly I've been trying to snag this for you."

She's begging like he hasn't been hounding her to get him

on *All Entertainment* for months. Should've smelled the day-old sushi right there. "Sure, Anj, set it up," he tells her. "I'm back from Tahoe on the fourth. . . ."

"No, Connor — ooh, don't kill me — but it's today. It's in two hours."

Connor must be firm about this; he cannot fold — he's entitled to a *life*. "Anjolie, I'm getting on a plane in two hours. . . ." Yeah, right, he's as firm as Grandpa without Viagra; he folds like fresh tortillas. She explains about the last-minute cancellation ("Jennifer Lopez got the flu! Connor, you're subbing for J.Lo!"), and he has to agree: You don't say no to the top-rated entertainment show on the tube. So he tells his boys the deal, they fly out without him — on his dime, no less! — and he humps over to the studio.

They do half a dozen takes before he realizes the faster he charms his way through it, the sooner he'll be perfecting his Burger Flip on the slopes. Done! So he swings by his condo to pack. Flinging this, that, and the other thing into a bag, grabbing clothes, CDs for the ride, and better not forget Lisle's Christmas gifts. He's hurrying, almost frantic — which makes no sense. It's a five-hour drive to Tahoe, so any way you look at it the day is shot. Yet it's the weirdest thing, he feels like he's running away from LA, running as if pursued.

Heavy, huh? Most actors are as deep as teacups but Connor, he's no shallow pretty boy. Maybe what's bugging him has to do with the way Olivia laid into him the other day.

Whatever, this feeling — big and dark and sort of foamy — is not cool. Anxiety, totally, but what does he have to worry about? His life is sweet. He pops a Xanax, tosses the vial in his toiletries bag. Then, as he goes for his car keys, Connor freezes. He grins. He knows what will fix his head, soothe his soul. Screw the Tank, he's not taking it. Up in Tahoe, it's an SUV beauty pageant. Connor knows what he needs — he needs a stick shift in his hand, man; he needs the top down; he needs some classic rock on the ster-ee-er-eo. He's taking the Bitch to Tahoe.

Scene VI: ELBOWS DEEP IN DOUGH

A kitchen is like a heart. This warm, wonderful notion occurs to Talisa DeLillo while she's in her kitchen, and she thinks it's not only wonderful and warm but oh so true. If she wasn't elbows deep in dough right now, she'd write it down, compose a poem around it, turn the poem into a song. But Talisa — a free spirit most of the time — is on a tight schedule. She can't be flittering off like a swallow to jot down a thought or toy with a tune. It's the morning of New Year's Eve, and Talisa's baking bread — twelve-grain with honey — to ring it in. Her mom used to do it, and her mom's mom before her, a tradition attached to mothers and daughters like patches in a quilt.

New Year's Bread. Twelve-grain for twelve months. Honey so that those months'll be rich and sweet. Bake this bread so the whole wide world — strangers and loved ones alike — can eat a slice on New Year's Day and not go hungry all year long. Of course the whole wide world is far from here, this lost place between mountains and sea. Yet Talisa bakes, and a song pops into her head, irrepressible, the melody poppy and pretty. She hums it, dances to it, too, bare feet slapping the stone floor, shoulders dipping as she kneads the supple substance on her wooden board.

Talisa's nose itches, tickled by a vinelike strand of dark hair escaped from her bandanna. She swipes it with the back of her wrist, knows she must have flour all over her face. The itch persists, and Talisa thinks: *Itch on, you can't stop me.* Since once the loaves are set to rise, she'll start on brownies and pie. And after baking, she'll cook. Pot of chili, vegetarian lasagna, a bunch of dips . . . festive food. Tonight, after all, is New Year's Eve. And even in a misbegotten place between a glittering seaside city and a sparkling mountain retreat, New Year's Eve always means a party.

Scene VII: TECHNICAL DIFFICULTIES

For the first leg of his journey, Connor's in crybaby mode — how bad does it suck to be driving solo when your buddies get to fly? An hour in, he actually begins to enjoy it. A guy as in-demand as Connor Moline doesn't often get time to himself. If he's not on set, he's doing interviews, or photo sessions, or walking the red carpet. Plus, the boys are around constantly, always crashing at his place. Besides, he's making tracks, the freeway moving — he'll be at the chalet soon enough.

Connor beats the steering wheel, smacking the rhythm to AC/DC's "Highway to Hell." A can of Red Bull rests between his legs — automotive designers didn't envision cup holders back in the Sixties, probably since the drive-thru concept as we know it was still way off. He ought to call Lisle, but where's his Sidekick? "Shit," Connor curses the wind in his face, keeping one eye on the road while rummaging in the glove compartment. Must have left the damn device in the Tank. Actually, that's cool. Something to be said about being so . . . incommunicado. Kind of Clint Eastwood badass cowboy, a real loner. When the Eagles' "Desperado" pours through his Blaupunkts, he sings along, loud and free.

But right then, when he's eased into laid-back mode, the car starts acting up. What, the Bitch doesn't like his voice? It begins with this slight grinding noise when Connor shifts gears, then she starts grinding at irregular intervals when he's not even touching the stick. Part of Connor immediately hits the panic button, but his sane side tells him: "Dude, please — chill."

"Look, you just had a tune-up with the anal-retentive mechanic," his sane side reasons. "It's just a glitch, some minor technical difficulty. Maybe she needs fluids. . . ."

Connor checks the dash — none of the dials are going apeshit or anything.

"Get off at the next exit, find a gas station," his sane side continues. "While they're putting oil in, or whatever, you can give Lisle a call."

Sometimes he makes so much sense! So although the next exit doesn't have one of those international gas symbol signs, Connor veers right and searches for a station along the two-lane blacktop. And searches . . . and searches. . . . And a thin trickle begins along the nape of his neck, a few beads on his forehead . . . And the Bitch grinds on, louder, more insistent . . . And there's nothing out here — nothing but saguaro and denuded bushes casting long shadows on the flat, endless land. . . . And who would have thought there are still places in America so devoid of civilization . . . And the sun is going down . . .

Finally, Connor spies a place, all by itself, miles from nowhere. Better not be a mirage! No, no, no — it's real: a puny two-pump station, a café behind it. It's a rundown, ramshackle place in dire need of a paint job, a neglected old house with a restaurant tacked to the front. The shutters on the café windows sag on their hinges, and signage that reads D ILL S is clearly missing a few letters. Whatever — he wants his car attended to, not a gourmet meal. As his wheels pass over a hose, a cheerful, reassuring *Ding! Ding!* announces his presence.

But no one hurries out to serve him. So Connor taps impatiently on his horn. Then taps again. Then leans on it.

Scene VIII: COLLISION COURSE

Now, that's unusual — it's barely eight o'clock, early for even the most ambitious New Year's revelers. Only some girls understand that nothing is unusual, and everything is unusual. The unexpected is always right on time, especially when perfect strangers are involved. Trouble is, this girl couldn't be less ready to entertain. She hasn't paid a thought to party attire yet, but two faded swaths of terry cloth definitely won't suffice. So, for the moment, Talisa does the only thing she *can* do: tightens her towels (one on her head, one around her torso) and pads — meanderingly, she's not about to run — downstairs to greet him.

Oh, whoever's out there is a *him*, all right. The way he has to toot his horn? Some show-off alpha male with a sense of entitlement — chest-beating gorilla, trumpeting macho mastodon. Fine, then — he'll have to take her as she is. She grabs the door handle, yanks . . .

Just as he, in a state of pique on the opposite side, shoves . . .

With a swoosh the two collide on the threshold. He: gripping her shoulders to stop a face-splat. She: leaning against him to prevent an ass-plop. She responds — immediately, accordingly — to the slapstick hilarity of the situation with a laugh like a silver hiccup. She is alone in this response.

"What — what's your *problem*?!" His face, an inch from

hers, turns several shades of magenta; his nostrils flare and his brows converge.

Ooh, the colors! Ooh, the contortions! "My problem?" Her wide blue eyes brim with mirth as she studies him.

"Yeah, you want to tell me what you're laughing at?" he demands.

"On what *planet* . . . is *laughing* . . . a *problem*?" The words burble at him. "But I'm . . . it's the way . . . do you know when you're mad, you turn purple?" And then she adds: "Whoever you are!"

What did she say? Every stupid messed-up thing Connor's had to deal with today fades as he fixes on those three little words — an outrage, the ultimate insult. He drops his hands and steps away. Maybe he didn't hear her right. Or maybe she needs glasses. Adjusting his stance, willing the hue of fury to drain, he tries on his trademark piercing yet sincere stare. *Go ahead, honey*, he thinks. *Take a loooong look. Let it sink in. Try not to pass out.*

And . . . nothing. Oh, she angles her chin slightly. Her giggles subside and she regards him, warm and even. But . . . *nothing.* Not a glimmer of recognition in those mountain-lake eyes. Unbelievable! Unless what's unbelievable is that he's here. Of course! Not in a million years would this boondocks babe even contemplate the possibility of him walking into her outhouse of a roadhouse. So he gives her a break. "I'm Connor Moline," he says.

The way he says it! Like "I'm Che Guevara," or "I'm John Lennon." A new barrage of giggles is set to launch but Talisa quells it, tilting her chin a bit more to express polite confusion. Tilts it too much, enough to topple her turban. Down comes half a mile of damp mahogany hair, smelling like mint and chamomile, billowing across porcelain shoulders all the way to her waist.

A sight to take a boy's breath away. Any boy. Every boy. Even a spoiled, jaded, been-there-hooked-up-with-that, hot-shot-from-Hollywood boy. So he does. Connor Moline can't help it. He gasps.

And she? She accepts his gasp graciously. Collects the undone towel in her hands, holds it unself-consciously at her side. "It's beautiful to meet you, Connor Moline." She says this because it *is* beautiful — but why, exactly, she isn't sure. Except it has nothing to do with the drape of his clothes, or the artisan-carved symmetry of his face, or any of the surface beauty she has already duly noted. That stuff is beside the point. The point is . . . something else. Something underneath his silly hubris and puffed-up posturing. And she intends to find it. So she smiles small and stands still. "I'm Talisa DeLillo," she says.

Scene IX: TINY PICKLE

"Connie! Connie, do you know what I am doing?" Lisle is happy to hear from her boy; she doesn't ask where he is or if he's all right — he is calling, so all is well in the universe that revolves around Lisle Blunke. "I am eating a pickle! A tiny little pickle, like my pinky . . . only wrinkly . . . and green."

Connor doesn't consider this information incidental or even inane; Lisle isn't a retard, just remarkably self-involved. "Yeah? Look, babe, you get in okay?"

"Yes, oh, the flight from New York was bumpy but I am fine now." Crunching delicately on her selection from the courtesy platter sent to the chalet by management, Lisle arranges her white-clad form on the white leather sofa in their suite. "Morgan told me you did a taping this morning. That is good, 'Star Chat' on *AE*. You go, Connie!"

"Yeah, well, J.Lo got the flu. . . ." Connor speaks absently into the clunky rotary phone, absorbing his surroundings — vintage jukebox; kaleidoscope of mismatched dishes behind the Formica counter; amazing mingle of aromas teasing through the porthole kitchen doors. He takes a brownie off a plate and bites into it — the girl, Talisa, she told him to help himself.

"I've got to go throw on some threads," she'd said. "Have a brownie, if you like. But hey, don't touch the bread! Can't eat that till New Year's Day." *What a weirdo, that one,* Connor thinks. *What's so special about some dumb loaf of bread?*

"Anyway," he tells Lisle, "look, I hit a snag, but nothing major."

"Uh-huh." Lisle is not really listening. Having dropped a

splotch of mustard on her Uggs, she's edging them off with her toes; fortunately, she packed a few pairs.

"Yeah, car trouble. Messed up, right?"

"Ooh, Connie? Which is the guy who is big with the studio? The one who shaves his head? Or the ugly one, DeLeon?"

Damn, Connor forgot all about Dylan Funtz! His boy Morgan wrote this killer script, a feature film vehicle for Connor as leading man. The plan is to pitch Funtz this weekend, and here Connor is — where the hell is he, anyway? — shit! "Dylan, he's Dylan," Connor corrects. "Look, Lisle, be extra nice to him till I get there, okay?"

No answer. Lisle is busy computing the caloric collateral damage of another pickle. She thinks she may have laced her bustier too tight, but doesn't want to change into something less enticing before meeting Morgan and DeLeon — oops, Dylan — in Snow Space, Tahoe's trendiest lounge.

"Leese? You there?"

"Yes, but ooh, Connie, I need to go. Okay? I see you very soon, yes? Kiss, kiss!"

Scene X: DEFINE ALONE

While Talisa's upstairs, getting dressed, Connor considers her . . . first impression. The image is pretty much burned on his retinas. Not that he hasn't seen plenty of girls in similar states: skimpy satin robes; coordinated contraptions straight out of a Victoria's Secret wet dream; stilettos, earrings, and not a stitch else. The difference, Connor muses, between those girls, all those girls, and this girl, is attitude. Your typical chick with the killer bod treats it like a trophy, a polished, exfoliated, Brazilian-waxed prize; she'll parade it, pose it, prop it up on velvet pillows. This girl, this Talisa, she's just cool with it, like: "Hi, I'm in a towel — hope you don't mind." Talisa in a towel — the most natural thing in the world. Weird. Weirder, she's . . . well, she's the kind of girl Morgan, smirk on stun, would call "healthy." In other words, not a stick. Morgan, with his smirks — if they gave out awards for being a prick . . .

Connor finishes his brownie, contemplates seconds, as Talisa descends. In a gauzy tunic, parchment colored, with voluminous sleeves and embroidery at the neck and hem, the outline of a camisole visible underneath. These flowy pants — low-slung, with tapestry panels in the wide bell bottoms. A fringed belt dangling from her hips. A strand of beads knotted at her heart. She still shuns shoes, coming toward Connor with her easy amble, tossing her hair — a hundred gleaming shades of brown, wavy as wood shavings — from one side to the other so she can fasten silver hoops in each lobe.

Putting the café counter between herself and Connor, she leans on her arms, studies him a second, then brushes brownie crumbs from the crook of his mouth with a fingertip. "You might want to take it easy with those," she says. "I forgot to tell you they're laced."

He doesn't want to blink — Connor Moline is an eye-contact expert, and it shouldn't be hard to let her gaze hold his, since it holds so gently, a caress, not a challenge. Still, Connor dips his lids, something unsettling in that caress. "What do you mean, laced?"

Talisa laughs. "Alice B. Toklas recipe," she says. "Infused by mood-enhancing ingredients from Mother Earth."

"Oh!" Connor gets it. "Space cakes. Cool." He's not a total stoner, but he can deal. "Let me tell you, lady, I could use a little mood enhancement about now. The day I had — insane." He shakes his head again, jogging his caramel curls. "So do me a favor, will you? Get your father or whatever grease monkey you got around here, stat, okay? I got pressing business in Tahoe and my car's giving me shit."

Talisa turns away, toward the coffeepots. "Can I pour you one?"

Java — just what Connor's jonesing for. "Absolutely," he says. "That's exactly . . . that'd be great. Leaded."

She sets a steamy mug before him, checks the contents of the tin creamer. Smiles as he adds milk, a spill of sugar. Stirs it up. Takes a sip. Smiles back. "Hey —" He almost says "hon" but stops himself. "Wow, good coffee, thanks. But look, um, Talisa? Can you just . . . you know, I'm really pressed for time . . ."

At that, Talisa lets loose one of her lilting giggles and glances quickly over his shoulder. "Time," she says. "Trippy, isn't it? The way we think it actually means something. Perhaps the most ludicrous mistake in the cosmos."

Connor has no clue what she means but her nonsense is a lullaby in an ancient language. It's nice, soothing; he could listen all night. Only suddenly, she gets real.

"Connor, I'm not sure I can help you," she says. "It's a bummer about your car, and I know you need to split, but my . . . I have . . . there's no mechanic here."

Wait, hold up, this is too bizarre. Maybe the brownie is starting to kick in. It dawns on Connor that this place is missing a lot more than a mechanic, yet he refuses to believe it. "Look, Talisa, get real," he says. "You can't be more than sixteen, seventeen tops, and you're trying to tell me you're alone here?"

Talisa shrugs. "Define alone."

Connor conks his forehead with the heel of his hand. "Alone. As in no parents and/or guardian. Aka family. And what about neighbors — look at this place, it's like a ghost town except there's no town . . . and no ghosts!"

Soon as the sentence pops out of his mouth, Talisa gets a funny little frown, then quickly replaces it with a smile. She notices that something has begun to come over Connor — he's not aware of it himself, but she can read it plain as a grocery list.

"As in what part of 'alone' don't you understand?" he continues, climbing off the counter stool, slipping into thespian mode. "As in De Niro going, 'Are you talking to me?' 'Cause I'm the only one here!'" Back on the stool, reaching across the counter, impulsively grabbing her hand. "It makes no sense . . . a girl like you . . ."

Her hand feels at home there. "A girl like me what?"

Abruptly, Connor realizes something. He realizes those are her actual eyelashes, thick and upswept, unadorned by mascara.

"It's . . . complicated," she says, then changes her mind. "No, it's not, it's irrelevant. I'm not alone because I don't feel alone. Just wait till later, you'll see."

See what? He's about to ask when she squeezes his hand. "Come on," she says. "I may not work for General Motors, but I'm a resourceful girl. Let's go look at your car."

Scene XI: UNHAPPY HOUR

"Liv-a-Snap?"

Olivia winces whenever one of the males in her family deems it fit to equate her with dog food. Her mother never called her that. Now her mother never calls her anything at all.

"I'm leaving, babydoll. . . ."

She winces anew, now that she's been compared to a plastic toy, or perhaps juvenile pajamas.

"Come on, give me a Happy New Year's hug."

Obediently, Olivia leaves her room to hug her father, off to pick up his date — a tanning-parlor technician from Orange

County — when what she really wants to do is slug him. Really, the man needs a good smack, the way you'd hit a hysterical person. Leather pants, hemp bracelets, spiked hair — someone needs to knock some sense into him.

"So what time is Anabeth's mom coming to pick you up?" he asks.

"Nine," Olivia lies. There is no Anabeth's mom. There is no Anabeth.

"And what are you girls going to get up to?"

"Nothing. Phony phone calls. Manicures." Olivia recites from a script her father will suspend his disbelief on. "Basic slumber party stuff."

He riffles the top of her head, encouraging further frizz. "Sounds like a blast. Don't forget to turn on the alarm when you leave. You know the code, right?"

"Right. Have fun, Dad."

"You, too, Snap." He hugs her. "Happy New Year."

His cologne is stultifying. "You, too."

He's gone, gone, gone, and she can breathe again. She puts her iPod in the docking station and cranks it. Then she walks into the kitchen and pulls out her party supplies: every single bottle of booze in the house. Arranges them alphabetically, Amaretto through Zima, on the kitchen island. Olivia assumed she'd always be Straight Edge, but screw it. She wants to get drunk. Wants to know how it feels. Be her own science project. She wants to lose control. Call it a New Year's resolution: "Get plastered!" So much more interesting than "Be a better person."

Scene XII: PITCH MEETING

"So what do you say, Lisle?"

That Morgan, he is always pitching. Lisle likes that about him. He is smart. And good-looking. Different from Connor, dark and rough. And Morgan is being attentive; Lisle likes attention, likes the way he shifts closer in his chair and puts one finger against the inside of her wrist. Morgan has a New Year's date — she's up in their room now, taking a pre-party power nap; Lisle is aware his attention is impure but basks in it nonetheless.

Morgan wants something. He's being very matter-of-fact about it, too, aiming to coerce her through inclusion. Do this, and you're one of us — not an outsider, not just some chick. Connor would want you to do it, even if he wouldn't say as much (and he *did* say be extra nice . . .). We're in this together, our eyes on the same prize — for Dylan Funtz to get his father to make the movie. These are the things Morgan suggests and implies and reminds while Dylan is in the men's room. Slowly, he draws a small circle inside Lisle's wrist, printing his mark with invisible, indelible ink.

True, there's a juicy role for Lisle in the movie Morgan wrote — the psycho zombie supermodel. But Dylan Funtz is not good-looking. It is funny, Lisle thinks, how it is so easy to do things with a guy who is good-looking and difficult to do the same things with a guy who is not. Not funny, but odd.

"In or out, Lisle?" Morgan cajoles. "Come on . . ."

He thinks he is so like Machiavelli. All his schemes. All his scripts. All his little maneuvers and side wagers. Yet as much as Lisle enjoys his persuasive purr and the patience of his circling finger, she is not so easy to manipulate, and she's as good at games as he is.

"I am sorry, Morgan, I see where you come from and I am not saying this is a bad idea, but I haven't decided." Lisle isn't mad that Morgan made the suggestion, she's simply not ready to commit to the performance he believes will slam-dunk the deal. "Maybe I will be in the mood later." She removes her wrist from Morgan's attempted spell and stretches both arms languidly over her head. With a flick of her eyes she sees Dylan Funtz — he is shaped like an egg, with a round middle and a pointy head — returning to the table. Being with him, convincing him she would *want* to — it would take a lot of acting talent to pull that off! Just the thought of doing it with Humpty-Dumpty almost makes Lisle laugh. Almost. Not quite. A tricky, malicious kind of laugh.

Scene XIII: UNDER THE HOOD

In one fluid motion Talisa slides out the dipstick like she's unsheathing a sword. She wipes it with a rag, examines the grease. "Well," she says. "You're not bleeding oil."

The light she's hooked to the open hood of Connor's car is garish; it shows how pale she really is, delineates the mole beneath the left edge of her lip. The mole is raised, like one of those candy buttons that come on white paper sheets — you peel 'em off, let 'em melt on your tongue.

"Yeah, well, I had an oil change a few weeks ago," Connor says, suddenly distracted as Talisa leans over the engine again, the edge of her tunic lifting to bare a glimpse of her smooth lower back, the lacy trim of her camisole. "Whatever, man, when I get back to LA I'm going to rip my mechanic a new one."

Using the rag, Talisa unscrews the radiator cap. "That's where you're from? LA?"

"Philly, originally, but we came to Cali when I was twelve," Connor says, still floored that Talisa doesn't know how huge he is. "You?"

"From back east, too," she says. "Massachusetts. Not that I remember; I was a baby when we moved here."

"Here. Ha!" Connor says. "Shit, what were your parents thinking?"

It's not a pretty tale but Talisa doesn't mind telling it. "Typical white-trash tragedy." She turns to lean against the car's gleaming flank. "There used to be some kind of plant out here — my dad had a steady job, and after a while, instead of buying a regular house, they invested in the café, since no one could cook like my mom. Well, the plant had troubles, my dad got laid off, and life around here was a carousel of fighting and drinking. Then Dad went out for the proverbial pack of cigarettes and never came back. But we got by; my mom did all right raising me and my brother —"

Connor interrupts: "You have a brother?" He uses the question as an excuse to move closer to Talisa; butts against the Bitch, they stare off into the fallen night.

"Teddy. He's three years older." Talisa squints, as if searching for a particular star. "He's in the war now. It's just incomprehensible — my sweet, funny, righteous brother in that awful, amoral war. . . ."

The way she trails off gives Connor the shivers. In his world, war is an Oliver Stone epic, Jake Gyllenhaal in combat costume, some grainy footage on The History Channel. Personally he doesn't know a soul who's off in Iraq, and to think Talisa's brother could be killed. It *is* awful — but what can he do, what can he say?

"Ohhh, uhhh, sorry," is all he can manage.

Talisa exhales heavily. Connor studies the sound of it, commits it to memory.

"You have any siblings?" she asks.

"Yeah, a sister," he says, adding, "she's just a kid."

Talisa looks at him, bittersweet-bright. "I bet she's crazy about you."

Loser bet, Connor thinks, turning to study the Bitch's mechanical guts so Talisa won't see his unease. But of course, she's Talisa — she senses it, letting her fingers rest against his. Ever so lightly, ever so poignantly. "So come on," Connor says, renewed by her touch. "Finish your dysfunctional family story."

Talisa waves off the notion. "Dysfunctional? Growing up with my mom? No, Connor. Our home, this café — our lives . . . we're all about music and art . . . and imagination, and exploration. I know you think this place, it doesn't compare to LA, but there's an energy here, and a pulse to our vibe, the things Mom nurtured in us — and because of that the most fabulous, fascinating people are drawn here." She pauses, gives him a tiny flip of lip. "After all, *you're* here, aren't you . . . ?"

Okay, this is nuts — how can he *not* be kissing her? And why does he feel like he wouldn't know how? Or is it that he's kissed too much, too often, too many mouths possessed by his for no other reason than that he could? As if his lips are tainted, he brushes them abruptly with the back of his hand.

That's when Talisa nudges him. "Start him up!" she says.

"Huh?" Just call him Connor the Clueless.

"Him." She indicates the driver's seat. "Don't you think it's sexist to automatically refer to cars as her?" Talisa's impish, not uptight. "This big, bad muscle machine — male, definitely."

Connor winces internally — if Talisa only knew he calls

the car the Bitch! But he obeys, turning the key in the ignition, letting the engine warm up, revving it — all to Talisa's direction. "There, you hear it!?" he bursts out when the Bitch starts bitching.

"Sure do," Talisa says. "You can turn him off now." Wandering into the garage, she tells Connor to hang on a sec. "That whiny grinding? Got to be transmission trouble," she says upon her return. "This is a quick fix, not a cure, but it'll get you to Tahoe." The plastic flask of Dexron is being difficult, the screw-cap stuck. "That's where you're headed, right? Tahoe?"

"Here, let me —" Connor reaches for it.

"It's cool, I've got —" Talisa struggles with the top.

It opens, all right. With a spew of viscous pinkish fluid all over her tunic.

"Oh, shit! Oh, Jesus! Oh, shit!" Connor's more upset about the accident than Talisa is. Way more.

"*Pfffft!*" She laughs. "Connor, it's okay — it's just a shirt." Nimbly she doses the Bitch. "That ought to do it," she tells him, eyes level. He's good to go, but she doesn't say it, and neither does he. Instead, she gazes down at herself. "I really am a mess, huh?" She unlatches the light, returns it to a hook in the garage, comes back to close the hood with a thud. They stand without speaking in the chilly starlight. And in another fluid motion Talisa strips off her shirt.

Scene XIV: DOMAIN OF A DEMIGODDESS

"Guess I better change into something less naked!" Talisa trills as she races toward the café.

Maybe a nanosecond passes before Connor races after her.

Flying her stained shirt like a banner, she whips it over her head and whoops. He's almost at her heels, trying to snatch it, as she leads him on a chase, behind the counter, serpentine through the tables, up the steps to the living quarters. At the foot of the stairs, Connor hesitates again — dare he enter her inner sanctum? Damn skippy! He takes them two at a time, but Talisa's already disappeared.

Tentatively, he tries a door in the murky hallway. He can barely make out the large four-poster, a few pieces of antique furniture, a painter's easel by the window. No Talisa. Down the hall, another door, another room. Clunky stereo, piles of vinyl records, bed in the corner. No Talisa. This door? A bathroom. And finally, no door but a sparkling beaded curtain.

"Welcome to my domain. . . ."

The room is lit by a tree lamp, three globes like glowing fruit. Exotic incense in the air — vanilla blended with an essence he can't identify. Some posters on the wall: Jimi Hendrix flagellating his Fender, Janis Joplin with flowers in her hair. Two dressers back to back in the center of the room, and from the ceiling, drapes of fabric — some heavy, velvet and brocade; some gauzy as veils — spill halfway to the floor to form a tent.

"In he-eeere . . ." Talisa entices.

Connor searches for an entrance to her hideaway, parts it with his hands. A pillow-strewn mattress atop the dressers — a makeshift loft — and in the middle, Talisa, legs fitted into a lotus, wearing only her camisole and the flowy pants. He is the desert wanderer, dying of thirst; she the odalisque of the oasis.

"Please . . ." she invites him, pure aural enchantment with a pinch of comedy. "*Do* come up."

He hoists himself, just shy of the mark, and must grapple with her many quilts and cushions. Giggling, she leans to help him; he flings a leg over. "Damn," he says. "That was . . . uh, athletic."

"You shall be rewarded for your efforts," Talisa promises. "Shoes, please!"

He kicks them off with a clunk onto the patterned carpet and settles into her warm, soft lair. "Oh, yeah? Lay it on me!"

Anticipation of her kiss — it feels like it's been with him a thousand years. Yet Talisa spins it out further, cruelly delicious. Unfolding herself, she stretches down over her loft and brings up a battered six-string. "For you, a serenade," she says.

"You play?" From the garage to the guitar — is there nothing this girl can't do?

"A little," she says, letting her feet dangle off the loft. "I just fool around, really. It's fun and it's . . . an outlet . . . for my feelings." She looks at her fret board, as if suddenly second-guessing this whole idea — this boy in her bed, this soul-baring song beating in her heart. Then she tosses her hair, and with it her doubt, striking a chord and soaring off with a translucent, confident soprano.

Connor's sure he's never heard the song, yet it's strangely familiar, the delicate melody, the lyrics about looking "at love from both sides now" and still not really understanding what it all means. Talisa messes up once, flubs a line, but it only serves to widen her smile — she can screw up in front of him and not be ashamed. As far as he's concerned, she could sing the phone book.

"Whoa," he says, as the last note resonates through the room. "That was awesome." The words have to climb the boulders in his throat. "Did you write that?"

Talisa laughs. "Yep, sure did — right after I painted the Sistine Chapel!" Carefully she leans over to place the guitar back in its stand. "That's Joni Mitchell, as if you didn't know."

So maybe he's not up on every up-and-coming indie singer chick. "Well, you sing it like it's yours — like you know what you're singing about."

A slight flush comes to her skin, abetted by a secret smile. "Mmm, sort of."

The more she alludes, the more he wonders. "Come on, Talisa, tell me," he plumbs her endless intrigue. "Have you . . . you know, 'looked at love from both sides now?'" Her expression is inscrutable — it's as if she knows, but she's not telling. "I mean, the whole love thing? Like what is it anyway?"

Talisa looks at him, half incredulous, half the opposite — expecting his ignorance. "Let me show you," she says.

Scene XV: WALK AWAY

There they recline, side by side in a fabric fortress, Talisa's camisole discarded, her pants gone to find it, Connor's shirt . . . someplace. How amazing to finally touch her, watch her move, hear her moan. The curve of her hips, the weight of her sloping breasts — so this is what a real girl feels like, a body minus the kickboxing and the silicone, multiplied by natural, unrelenting passion. Her whispers between kisses, her giggles and sighs of pleasure as they slowly explore — alcove of armpit, miles of spine, the tremble-inducing texture of a nipple against his cheek, his fingers, his tongue. They have all night, they have all year, they have forever.

Until the blasts of a horn invade their bliss. And Talisa draws herself agonizingly away from him. "To be continued . . ." she says as she slips away.

"Wait . . . Talisa, come on, don't go . . ." He reaches for her. "Whoever it is, they'll go away."

Now a sigh mixes with a giggle — resigned yet delighted. "Ooh, Connor . . . you can't interrupt destiny." She slides down from the loft, slips into her clothes.

Next thing Connor knows, they're downstairs, Talisa being

swallowed by a swarm. Vintage cars and vans pulling up to the café, kids of all colors piling out. Talisa calling greetings, doling out embraces. One guy — his red hair and beard shaggy, his green eyes glinting — grabs her and swings her around.

"Joe!" Talisa cries. "It's been so long — too long." Linking her arm through Joe's, she navigates the crowd. Conner sees them coming toward him and he tenses. *Who is this dude?*

"Conner, meet Joe," she says. "He's the grooviest guy on the planet and my brother Teddy's best friend."

"Hey man," says Joe, sizing Conner up — making sure he's worthy of the sweetness in Talisa's smile, the kiss-flush in her face.

"Hey, good to meet you," Conner says, holding Joe's gaze, level, steady, and true. Apparently Conner passes the test, because Joe gives him a nod, followed by a grin.

"Oh, look, it's Star!" Talisa says excitedly at the sight of another New Year's celebrant, and takes off.

Conner lets her go — it's as wonderful to watch her from afar as to be by her side. . . well, almost. What can he do now but mingle.

Talk about a time warp. The air pungent with a familiar funky smell. Kinks and Stones spewing from the jukebox. The way everyone's tricked out — flares and fringe, paisley and Day-Glo, all the wild hair — it could be a masquerade ball, but Connor's on point. Occasionally he and his boys slum in the Silverlake neo-hippie scene — boho's no biggie; he's seen it all. It's just his fierce yet futile wish that this raging throw-down were taking place in LA, or anywhere other than this café. If he had his way, he and Talisa would be partying *à deux*.

Everyone at DeLillo's seems astoundingly chill about the celebrity presence, though, and that irks him. Not to be paranoid, but sometimes people play dumb to who you are out of jealousy. Connor's glad there's not a lot of drinking going on — alcohol has a way of stoking hostility, so it wouldn't take too many cocktails for things to get nasty.

No sign of that so far. People are dancing freestyle, scarfing Talisa's culinary delights. Connor roves the room, looking for her in the crowd. For a second he'll think he hears her laughter or whiffs the fresh scent of her hair, and he'll turn in that direction but it will be gone. He needs to find her.

The jukebox is berserk, six tracks for a quarter, but eventually it runs out. Acoustic guitars, tambourines, a host of improvised instruments fill the sonic void. Four girls do a sped-up spiritual while somebody strums. One guy shoots for a free-rap thing over slurry bottleneck slide. Then a chant catches fire: "Tah-*lee*! Tah-*lee*!"

Here she comes, looking a little flustered while the red-haired guy, Joe, and a tall, skinny dude with an afro as wide as an archway hoist her onto a tabletop, hand her a guitar.

"This is silly!" she protests. "I've got guacamole to mash!"

The assemblage starts clapping, throwing out requests.

"Do 'Piece of My Heart!'"

"Do 'Fire and Rain!'"

"No, come on, Tali," says Joe. "Give us an original."

Connor can't get any closer to her table, but he's near enough to see the faint pink of her blush and the excited spark in her eyes.

"Okay, you lunatics!" Talisa says. "Let me see. Okay, here's one. This is about the options you have when love does you wrong. It's called 'Walk Away.'"

A sprite melody belies the upheaval of betrayal, and Talisa fingerpicks expertly, like she could do it in her sleep. Her voice revealing a deeper level of her range, a rolling contralto with a touch of torch, and she brings it poignantly, because she's stood in that painful place — and walked away. And she looks so heart-wrenchingly beautiful, from the first note to the last, Connor wishes she *would* walk away — from this crowd, this café, this entire realm of existence — with him at her side.

Scene XVI: ON A TRAJECTORY

Two girls are feeling ugly. Two girls are making themselves sick — there's no one else to blame, no one is forcing them, they know this — yet they won't turn back. They have made a decision. They have a trajectory. And it's not even midnight.

One girl's in a sprawling split-level ranch house in that part of LA known as the Valley. She has reached the letter "C." But she can't figure out how to pop champagne, which

would at least be appropriate. Nor can she master the cork-
screw, so Cabernet is also out. That leaves her with Courvoisier.
It tastes like rancid molasses mixed with Listerine, and on top
of the sweet Amaretto and the bitter beer, it makes her beeline
for the bathroom. The first heave seems to come from as far as
her heels.

The other girl is in a postmodern ski chalet in Lake Tahoe.
She is not becoming intoxicated alphabetically. She sticks to
her favorite C: champagne. Something about it makes you feel
you can get away with anything, that nothing matters. Like
Connor — he's here, he's not here, what's the difference? It's
all a game. And she's had just enough bubbly to play. She
giggles aloud, but the giggle turns into a burp as she totters
toward the couch and asks someone to scoot over.

There are six, maybe eight other people in the room. The
more, she thinks, the merrier. Depravity demands spectators.
The music is all beat and syllables, nonsense lyrics, but she
understands as she leans into the ear of Dylan Funtz, this
moment's leading man, and tells him a secret, a secret that's all
tongue and no language. Members of the audience relinquish
ringside seats on the couch — a little too close for comfort — but
don't go too far. They want to watch. Lights, camera, action.

Scene XVII: SILLY, USELESS TIME

The year is running out. Heads or tails, beginning or end?
There are deals to make, and promises; there is peace to make,

too. Tomorrow, yesterday, and this very second all spin simultaneously while a party careens toward the manic point. A blond boy with twenty-twenty vision feels blinded by the smoke in the room, the roar in the room, the essences, gyrations, hits and fits and misses. Connor goes outside, turns his back to bacchanal, his eyes to the land and sky. He'll do it, just do it; he'll leave without good-bye. Of course he won't; he'll stand there, and if he's lucky, really lucky, he'll cry.

Then he hears a sound. Not the contained cacophony of the party. It's outside. Out here. An eerie, persistent creaking. Simply wind in a tree? Or someone sinister creeping around? Connor's dramatic instincts lock and load — he's scared, but if it's a bad guy, he's propelled to play hero. Breath tight, tread cautious, he starts off to investigate. There, behind the café, his fear falls away like sand, and he races up to the swing set where Talisa, all by herself, tries to kick the moon.

"Hey . . . !" he shouts.

She looks at him, hair flying. "Wheee!"

Taking a seat on the swing next to her, he pumps hard, but cannot match her rhythm — she's up, he's down. But when she slows, he leaps off his swing, goes behind hers and holds her chains from behind. "Gotcha!"

Talisa lets herself fall back against him. The beat of his heart is strong and resolute.

"You had to get out of there too, huh?" he asks, his mouth

adrift in her wealth of dark waves, near to the delicate skin of her throat. "What a nuthouse!"

She giggles. "Imagine if I actually invited people!"

Connor clings to the chains of her swing, as if he has any control at all. "I thought I lost you," he says, and once he has admitted this, the words hover like spirits. So he chases them off with inconsequential observation: "Hey, you're wearing shoes."

She sticks out her feet, exhibiting them like a little girl in new Mary Janes.

"I didn't know Talisa DeLillo *did* shoes," he adds.

Actually, they're chunky platform boots, and she's also donned a long coat, some feathery substance wisping from collar and cuffs. "Only on special occasions," she says, then springs off the swing. "Hey, you want to see something?" Like he has a choice but to follow her . . . anywhere? She jogs a few steps backward. "Come on, it's only half a mile or so."

Snatching his Volcom parka from the car, he catches up to her. They don't speak much along the way, listening instead for some lesson in the night. They traipse from the flats to the foot of the mountains. And in this mountain, a cave. And in this cave, every niche and nook has a candle. And every candle has a flame.

Connor is capable of one thing: awe.

Talisa's giggle echoes softly. "I'm the same way — even though I've been here a million times," she says. "My mom found this place. It's where she'd go when things got bad. It's where I go . . ." She takes his hand. "Come, look, we can sit." They find a sofa made of stone lined with a sturdy sleeping bag. "I like to bring my guitar here; the acoustics are crazy. Sometimes I play, sometimes I write, sometimes I just . . . think, and dream . . . oh, Connor, am I babbling?"

He still can't form words, but her words, whatever she says, are a symphony to him as they fit together, arm over shoulder, head to chest. The silence they lapse into is special, but Connor has to find his voice again. He wants to kiss her again, but first there are things he has to ask, things he has to say. "Your mom," he begins. "She — she's dead, isn't she? You really are alone. . . ."

Talisa yearns for the things he has to ask, the things he has to say. "Yes, Connor. My mom died. I am, by your definition, alone."

"Not anymore . . ." Never has a murmur meant so much. "I mean, Talisa — you really don't know who I am?"

She pokes him in the ribs. "Of course I do — you're Connor Moline!" she says. "You're from Philly, you live in LA, you've got business in Tahoe . . . but right now you're with me." She snuggles against him. "What else could I possibly need or want to know?"

A lot! Everything! "Well, I'm . . . for one thing, I'm an actor. Obviously your mom didn't think too highly of television —"

"The opiate of the people —"

"But I'm on TV. Every week. I'm . . . damn it, I'm a TV star. I'm famous. And, Tali, look — please, *please* don't think I'm an asshole — but I make a shitload of money; I've got a great apartment. . . . And you can . . . you can come with me. Come with me to Tahoe; come with me to LA. Come with me, Talisa. Be with me."

He hears himself saying this and knows how right it is.

"Connor, you feel okay?" she teases him. "You don't sound like you."

No joke. "That's because I'm a completely different person," he says.

"Oh, no, you're not," she counters quietly. "You're . . . it's like being on the swing. Back and forth, crazy high, snapped back — it takes a while to get centered. You're not a different person, Connor, it's just . . . tonight you fell into place." She cranes her neck to gaze at him. "You're the person you're supposed to be. But you had to get lost to get found."

He cups her face with his palm. "You're a real know-it-all, aren't you? Well, let me tell you something you *don't* know."

"What, that it's New Year's?"

"Wait — what? It is?" He looks at his watch. "Wow — almost . . ." Quickly he shifts position so they can both see the second hand sweep. "Okay," he whispers. "It is now . . . officially . . . Happy Newwww . . . Year."

A single silvery chime emits from his silly, useless, expensive timepiece. And as he brings his lips to hers, she meets him. And as he loses his hand in her hair, she meets him. And as he allows his eyes to close, she meets him. And with lips touching, hands lost, and eyes closed, they are everywhere and everyone and always all at once.

"So are you going to tell me?" she wants to know, after a while.

Oh, yes. He's going to tell her everything. "Tell you what?" he asks.

"That 'something I don't know'?"

He can't stop smiling. It's like his face is deliriously possessed. And his body is enveloping a girl from a dream — the girl of his dreams. And his senses revel in her essence, her glow, her heat. Words he's heard uttered in a million movies that never made sense before now occur to him with brilliant clarity. This is not a line — not this time. This is the flesh-and-blood Connor Moline talking, not cinematic stud puppy Danny Stiles. This is no lie. This is truth. Pure, perfect truth. "Oh," he says. "That's easy. I love you. I'm in love with you. Talisa, I love you."

She doesn't say it back. She lets it settle over the both of them like a cloak. She lets it fill the space around them and spar with countless candle flames. Then she parts her lips, inhales his exhales, and kisses him again. And again and again.

When he reminds her that she hasn't given him an

answer — about coming with him, about being with him — she kisses him again. And again and again.

And just as he falls asleep, she snuggles deeper into his strength — the safety of his arms, the armor of his chest, the steady insistence of his heartbeat. "I love you, Connor," she says. "I love you, too." And she kisses him one more time.

Scene XVIII: LIGHT OF DAY

When Connor stirs, hours later, he's alone — but not alarmed. Talisa isn't in his arms, but he can sense her around him, sweet as the air. All the candles have gone out, but there's dim light at the mouth of the cave. Must be morning. Connor heaves himself into it, not even compelled to call her name — she's still here, with him.

He checks his Rolex. Three-fifteen?! No way, bay-bee. The sun has claimed the horizon, it's definitely past dawn. And it's gorgeous out. So gorgeous Connor couldn't care less that his 10K watch has stopped. Stepping outside, he feels like a wild man, the first man, man reborn. He doesn't need to get his bearings — knows exactly where he is, and which way to the café. Talisa probably slipped off to pack a basket with coffee, some of that mystical New Year's bread she'd alluded to the day before. That would be just like her. And it would be just like him to meet her halfway.

He gets halfway — and doesn't meet her. He gets three-quarters of the way — and doesn't meet her. Now Connor quickens his pace. The café comes into view; he can see the swing set, silent now, and still. Going around to the front, there's the Bitch right where he left her, the other cars from last night absent. But in the dawn light, the place looks renewed, as if it's finally had a fresh coat of paint. And the sign reads DELILLO'S — what, did someone take a ladder and fix it as a New Year's present to Talisa? Weirder still, that strip mall across the road. Connor hadn't noticed it when he drove up yesterday — it's as though the Staples and Target erected themselves overnight, mushrooms after a rain.

Connor enters DeLillo's Café, but the name in his heart stops short on his tongue. The aftermath of a party surrounds him — bottles and glasses scattered, an abstract painting of drips on the floor. The smell of brewed coffee, a servant of the new day, valiantly chases the dregs of night. Connor decides to go behind the counter, help himself to a mug, just as the kitchen doors swing open.

A man's thickly muscled back appears, and when the guy turns around he's loaded down with a rack of cups and saucers. An old guy, an apron over his T-shirt and jeans. His arms are heavily tattooed; gray streaks in his ponytail. "Oh!" Surprised to see Connor standing there, the guy quickly collects himself. "Hey, kid." He nods toward the stools. "The tables are still a wreck — kind of a barn burner in here last night — but have a seat at the counter, I'll be right with you."

Connor, stupefied, slo-mo, sits.

The guy unburdens himself of wet-from-the-dishwasher china and lumbers up. A big man, his eyes are deep and blue, troubled but not unkind. "What'll it be?"

"I — uh — um . . ." Connor's mouth is thick with sludge, his thoughts are confetti. "Coffee . . . please . . ." he finally orders, hoping caffeine will bring clarity. He takes a few sips while the counterman goes about his business. "Hey . . . mister?" Connor calls out.

"You want something else?" the old guy says.

"I'm actually — I came in, I'm looking for someone," Connor says. It should be easy. Just ask for Talisa. Talisa DeLillo. Bewildered as he is, and so much in need of an answer, the words still seem to stick in his throat. "Someone I met . . . I was here last night, there was — this girl."

A toothpick has appeared in the old guy's mouth; it works its way from one side to the other. "Yeah, there were some kids here, but I don't remember you."

"Well, I was here," Connor insists. "And this girl, you must know her, she's a — she's really great-looking, with blue eyes and long dark hair . . . and she's got a beauty mark, like a candy button, right here." Connor touches his own chin.

The counterman's eyes go from liquid to stone. "There was no one here like that," he says and turns away.

"But —" Connor says, just as a new customer walks into the café.

"Hey, Teddy." The newcomer takes a seat without a glance Connor's way. "You get any sleep?"

The counterman pours a cup without being asked. "Hell no, Joe," he says. "Running on fumes. Fried egg on a roll?"

Joe? Connor studies the newcomer. Another old dude. Reddish crewcut. Coveralls. *"Joe . . . ?"* The name escapes.

"Yeah?" Joe still has a baby face. "Heyyyy," he says, and his smile is genuine. "I know you!" He strolls his cup down a few stools, then sits next to Connor. "Wait, don't tell me." He slaps the Formica with work-gnarled fingers. "That's it! My granddaughter, she's crazy about you. You're that kid from *Peanut's Point!*"

Connor coughs. *"Pinot's . . ."* he says weakly.

"Teddy! Hey, Teddy, this kid's famous," Joe shouts. "He's on TV!"

Glowering, Teddy puts a plate in front of Joe, returns to the kitchen. Joe smiles. It's a smile Connor knows well. Somehow he returns it. "Yeah, you got me." Connor lifts his coffee cup. Joe raises his for a clink. Two conspirators, buddies from back in the day. Perked by his coffee, amped by his eggs, Joe begins a reminiscent ramble about his younger days — the bashes they threw, the girls he knew. Quite a talespinner, that Joe; a screenwriter without a script, sucking Connor in. *It's as if I'm there*, Connor thinks, *the music, the mood.* Then two words slip unbidden from his lips. "And . . . Talisa?"

Joe screws up his face. "Talisa?" A soft, low whistle sneaks from between his teeth as he steals a glance toward the kitchen doors. "You've . . . seen her?"

Connor leans closer, almost hisses: "Last night!"

Joe nods. "It happens," he says, "from time to time. But you don't want to say anything to Teddy. It . . . ah . . . really upsets him." Joe mumbles the last line into his cup.

Connor wonders if a few screws have loosened up since he last saw Joe. After all it's been, what, thirty, forty years? "But you can tell *me*, Joe . . ."

"Well, I blame that guy," he confides, biting into his sandwich. "You're not from around here, you wouldn't know him — local hero, talented, I'll give him that, thought he was the golden-haired Bob Dylan, the next Gram Parsons. But you know" — he swipes errant egg with a napkin — "kind of a shitbird. Full of himself. Didn't stop Tali from falling for him, though.

"It's like she had to see under that stuff, always looking for the reason why, like if she found it — what made you a jerk — exposed it, it would go away." Joe takes another mouthful. "But man, sometimes an asshole is an asshole is an asshole. So that time, at the party — goddamn, if it wasn't forty years ago last night! — she caught him with his hand up some other girl's skirt . . . and she just, well, she walked away. Off into the night. Probably headed to that cave she liked to hide out in . . ."

Joe checks furtively for Talisa's brother once more. "That's when the drunk driver — poor dumb slob got twenty-five for vehicular manslaughter, died up in Folsom before he was even eligible for parole. Well, a state trooper discovered the . . . not a scratch on her, not even her clothes messed up. Time of death, they said, three-fifteen A.M. . . ."

Hearing this, Connor's heart seems to stop, just like the workings of his Rolex. But his mind keeps going, and on its screen he sees himself walking along that road, way back then, discovering his love like a fallen bird, kneeling down . . .

"And the guy, the asshole whose name I'm happy I forgot, he left town and no one ever saw him again — not on an album cover, either, that's for sure," Joe says bitterly. "But the worst was Teddy, man, he never recovered. First his mother, this truly beautiful lady, they bring him back from Nam so he could bury her . . . and then, months later, his baby *sister* . . ."

Connor blanches under his tan. His hands can no longer hold his cup. But somehow the pump of his pulse is stronger than ever. He believes — the impossible, the incredible. He slips on acceptance like a battered pair of Adidas.

With a slurp, Joe finishes his coffee. He pulls out his wallet and slaps some crinkled bills on the counter, then slides a napkin toward Connor. "Hey, you think you could autograph this? For my granddaughter?" Connor doesn't object, so Joe takes a pen from his coveralls. "Make it out to Lacey, okay? That's L-a-c-e-y."

Robotically Connor scribbles *Dear Lacey, See ya at the Point.* Then his signature, with a practiced, flourished slant.

"Thanks a lot, she's going to be thrilled!" Joe says. "Hey, by the way, Happy New Year!" He turns to go, but doubles back to stare once more into Connor's stricken face. "When you . . . with Tali . . ." he begins. "Did you happen to tell her you loved her?"

The memory of the moment swells up inside him. "Yes," Connor says hoarsely. "I did. I — I . . . I do."

"You did," repeats Joe. "You do." He looks at Connor, looks into him. "I'm glad. Because she deserved the best, she really did." He turns his gaze to the window, to the beautiful brand-new day. "Maybe that's all she needed to hear. . . ."

Scene XIX: THE END

The Bitch is being a good girl, lapping up the road like a kitten. Connor Moline, TV star, "It" Boy, drives with the top down, one finger on the steering wheel. Ten miles over the speed limit — acceptable. He wonders what he will tell her, how much he will tell her: *I just spent the most amazing night of my life with a girl who's been dead forty years. So how was your New Year's?* Maybe he won't have to say a thing — he feels so different, so transformed, maybe it will show; she'll take one look at him and know.

He pulls in, strides through the door, allowing long beams of light to infiltrate the shades-drawn room. He hears music:

Black metal assault, jarring, pummeling, the guitars going *digga-digga-digga*. Where is she? There's no sign of her, no indication of human existence. Until he finds her crumpled on the couch. In three steps he's there, and kneeling, carefully peeling hair from her moist face. "Olivia!" he calls out, pats her cheeks. "Liv! Liv!"

Her eyelids, swollen as leeches, struggle to slit. "Uch!" she says. "Connor?" She tries to elbow herself erect, fails miserably. He helps her to upright, sits beside her.

"What happened here?" he doesn't ask.

"What are you doing here?" she doesn't ask.

A new song comes on — some mopey emo tune. Olivia sniffs and hawks. "Uch . . ." comes out of her again, unbidden.

"You need to hurl?" he strokes her hair. "You want me to help you to the bathroom?"

Lightly, hesitant, she leans her head on his chest. It's solid, warm. She shakes her head against it. "Did enough of that last night," she croaks, glancing up at him.

"I'm glad you're here," she doesn't need to say.

"I'm glad I'm here, too," he doesn't need to say.

Instead he asks, "You want to go get something to eat?"

She rolls her eyes painfully. "I don't think I could . . ."

He stifles a knowing laugh. "Just wait till you smell toast, you'll be ravenous. We could go to The Curious Farmer." Always was her favorite place, since when she was little. "I've been there, Liv." He means hungover, not The Curious Farmer. The barest smile tries to push up the corners of her mouth. "Many a time," he adds. "Trust me."

The smile wobbles into place. "Mm-kay," she says. "If you say so."

Cold water, the miracle of toothpaste, bring Olivia back to life. She pulls on a baseball cap, and Connor takes her jean jacket off a hook in the front hall, handing it to her. The sun outside is blinding. The temperature is already seventy-two idyllic degrees.

Climbing into the Bitch, Olivia finds a package — brown wrapping, tied up with string — lying on the passenger seat. It's pliant in her hands, and it smells like heaven. "What's this?" she asks Connor.

"No clue." He won't permit his wet-threatened eyes upon the humble gift.

Olivia pulls the string and the paper falls open. There, mute and tempting in her lap, a golden loaf of home-baked bread, the most natural thing in the world.

✳ ✳ ✳ ✳ ✳ ✳ ✳

THE CHRISTMAS CHOOS

✳

Melissa de la Cruz

✳ ✳ ✳ ✳ ✳ ✳ ✳

"There he is," Kelsey Cooper said, spotting her boyfriend's shaggy dark head above the crowd of people exiting the annual "Joy to the World: Parker High Christmas Concert Extravaganza." "Over here!" she called, waving her program in the air. Her breath caught in her throat the same way it did every time she saw him.

Tall, broad-shouldered, and still tan from working outdoors in his grandparents' apple orchard during the autumn harvest, Brenden Molloy had cheekbones to rival Orlando Bloom's and blue-green eyes that sparkled with wicked fun, and he would be the cutest guy in school if it weren't for tousled bangs that obscured half of his face. His hair was so long it curled underneath his ears and licked his shirt collar.

He shot her a quick grin as he walked over to Kelsey and her friend Gigi McClusky, taking graceful, loping strides, cradling his saxophone in its black case.

Instead of saying hello, Kelsey rushed up and pushed his hair back from his forehead.

"Hi to you, too," he teased.

Kelsey sighed. Brenden had looked so nice earlier in his concert uniform — a black tuxedo — and part of her secretly wished that he could look like that all the time: not necessarily in black tie, but just a bit more polished and cleaned up than usual. He had already changed into his usual attire of holey Arctic Monkeys T-shirt, battered jean jacket, weathered cotton Dickies, and thick-soled black combat boots. With his messy hair and collection of thick black armbands, he looked seriously grungy. Hot, but grungy.

In contrast, Kelsey was meticulously put together, as if she'd stepped off the pages of a glossy magazine, from her seashell-pink manicure to her tailored fur-trimmed red car coat. She was slim, with fair, clear, cornflower-blue eyes, burnished, honey-brown hair with strawberry-blonde highlights, and skin that tanned easily during the summer, sprinkling freckles across her nose and cheeks. Like Brenden, she was sixteen years old, and a junior at Parker.

"You were awesome!" Kelsey beamed. Brenden was first-chair saxophone — a big deal, since six kids who played the same instrument had vied for the same spot.

"Bravo!" their English teacher Mrs. Townsend interjected as she passed by, smiling warmly at Brenden. The Christmas recital was a town favorite — even the mayor never missed a performance.

"Yeah, cool *solo*," Gigi drawled, although from her tone of voice it was obvious that she thought playing the interlude to "White Christmas" for the school orchestra was far from "cool."

"Thanks," Brenden mumbled, looking down at his boots.

Kelsey glanced from her boyfriend to her friend with a rising feeling of panic, wishing that they would miraculously find some way to get along. She should have known it had been a mistake to invite Gigi to the concert.

Gigi McClusky was the head of the Wade Hill crowd, a group of rich, snobby kids who all lived in the same ritzy part of town and had all attended the same small, private elementary school within the gated community. They were traditionally sent to boarding schools back east to prep for college, but recently a large, and growing, contingent were sent to Parker High. Until they'd arrived, Kelsey had never known there was anything wrong with her JC Penney wardrobe, her dad's ten-year-old Chrysler, or her Delia's backpack. But the Wade Hill kids were dropped off in their parents' BMW SUVs, shopped at Saks Fifth Avenue in the mall, and toted bags made of calfskin instead of canvas.

They had welcomed Kelsey into their ranks even though Kelsey wasn't rich, snobby, or from Wade Hill. (Her fur-trimmed coat was a knockoff.) But she was prettier than the whole lot of them put together, and after all, they couldn't call themselves the Beautiful People if they didn't count the most beautiful girl in school among them.

Kelsey laced her arm through Brenden's and gave it a squeeze. She would rather have kissed him but knew he was slightly embarrassed by PDA. He rarely even held her hand when they were out together. She wished he would be more demonstrative in public, although he more than made up for it when they were alone.

"Seriously, Bren, you guys rocked," she said, a little too enthusiastically, hoping to smooth over Gigi's passive-aggressive dis.

"Yep, we turned it all the way up to eleven," Brendan deadpanned, making a reference to their favorite movie *This Is Spinal Tap*. The image of the Parker High orchestra populated by aging British metalheads made Kelsey giggle, and soon she and Brenden were laughing at the shared joke while Gigi stood uncomfortably to the side.

"Well, I should go!" Gigi announced abruptly. "I told my dad I'd be home early tonight. There's so much work we still need to do for the party!" She tossed her long, black, Jordana Brewster-meets-Demi Moore hair over her shoulder. "Bye-yee," she said, leaning over and affectedly kissing the air two inches away from each of Kelsey's cheeks while Kelsey did the same to her. "Mwah! Mwah!"

Brenden tried not to roll his eyes. "Tell me again how you can stand her?" he grumbled, as they walked out of the auditorium through the revolving glass doors to the parking lot.

"She's my *friend*," Kelsey said tightly. "She's *nice* to me."

He shrugged, dropping the subject for once, and Kelsey was relieved. Brenden thought Gigi was a shallow airhead and typically didn't hold back from telling Kelsey so, but it was too beautiful an evening for quarreling. Outside, a pristine blanket of snow covered everything from the old slate shingles on the building rooftops to the surrounding meadows and towering fir trees. The air smelled fresh and brisk, scented by the earthy, rich fragrance of pine.

"I love it here." Kelsey sighed.

There was nothing special about Parker, Ohio — it was such a small town that its main drag consisted of a lone bank, beauty salon, and pizza parlor, as well as the three squat buildings that made up the entire public school system. An hour and a half away from Cleveland and forty-five minutes from the nearest mall, its most famous resident was a girl who'd tried out for *American Idol* last season but got cut on the first round. But every year during Christmas, Kelsey thought it was the best place in the world.

Across the street from the high school, the little wooden gazebo in the middle of the town square was decorated with evergreen garlands heavy with red holly berries and white mistletoe sprays. An enormous wreath festooned with silver pinecones hung over the entrance to the City Hall, and twinkling white lights wrapped around the candy-cane-colored barbershop poles added to the festive sight.

"It looks like a Hallmark card," Kelsey said. "In a good way."

"You say that every year." Brenden smiled.

"I know, but it's true."

Brenden nodded at the wisdom of that statement. "Hey,

what's over there?" he asked, putting his saxophone case on the ground and motioning toward the distance. Kelsey swiveled to look to where he was pointing, only to feel a shock of something cold and wet on the back of her neck.

"Oh, no, you *didn't!*" she squealed, shaking the snowball off. She immediately scooped a handful of snow with her gloved hands and plastered him in the face with it. Brenden hopped away, but Kelsey had a good arm and had soon pelted him with a half-dozen snowballs.

"Truce! Truce!" Brenden yelled, laughing hysterically as a volley of snowballs struck his torso. "I know you love to win."

"Remember in third grade when I put that walkie-talkie in your closet?" Kelsey said. "You thought your GI Joes were talking to you!"

"Remember in fifth grade when I hid that frog in your lunchbox?" he taunted, packing a snowball and aiming for her pitching arm. "You screamed for a week!"

"Did not!" she howled, momentarily rendered off-balance by his offensive strike. She scrambled onto the snowbanks to collect more ammunition.

They reached the far side of the school parking lot, still throwing snowballs at each other, and Brenden looked around to see if anyone was nearby. Once he'd confirmed they were alone, he grabbed Kelsey by the waist and pulled her down to the snow with him, the two of them tumbling on the ground and laughing.

"There," he said, brushing the snow off her hair.

"Let go." She laughed breathlessly, feeling the weight of him on her body, keeping her warm.

"No way." He shook his head. He put his arms and legs on top of hers, and began to wave them up and down to make a snow angel.

"Stop it — that tickles!" Kelsey said, feeling the cold start to seep through her coat and sweater. But for once she wasn't worried about how her hair or her clothes looked. Brenden was the only guy she'd ever known who could make her laugh so hard her belly ached. "It's cold out here!" she gasped as a light snow began to fall, and the glow from the streetlights turned each snowflake into a flickering beacon.

In answer, Brenden leaned over her so that their faces were so close to each other that she could feel his breath on her cheek. "Still cold?" he whispered, his eyelashes fluttering on her forehead, his fingers intertwining with hers, and his legs straddling her own.

"No . . ." She lifted her lips up to him for a kiss, and their mouths met, open and wet, and she could taste snowflakes on his tongue.

"You love me, Kelseygirl?" he asked, looking deep into her eyes.

"I love you, Brenden James Molloy," she whispered, pulling him closer so he could hear.

"Good, because I love you, too." He grinned, getting up and lifting her to her feet.

The very first time they'd kissed was one afternoon last summer when they were shooting hoops in Brenden's backyard. After he'd made several over-the-shoulder alley-oops to flatten her 16-4, he'd turned to her and said, ultracasually, as if he were perusing a menu and ordering a hamburger, "I really like you." She'd blushed and said she didn't know what he was talking about; of course they liked each other — they were friends. They'd spent their childhoods bickering and teasing each other. Brenden had seen her sick with the chicken pox when they were five, and a few years later she was the only one who knew Brenden had cried when his parents split. So she didn't know what he was getting at until he put the basketball down and looked at her straight in the eye.

"No, I mean, I *like you* like you," he'd explained. Then he'd kissed her while the sun set behind the ravine and he smelled like Trident gum and Red Bull and tasted like something infinitely more delicious — like chocolate and boy-sweat, salty and sweet. It was the first and best kiss of her life. They were like Jennifer Garner and Mark Ruffalo in *13 Going on 30*, except they hadn't needed any magic wishing dust or a New York City idyll complete with Michael Jackson "Thriller" dance moves to find each other.

Now Brenden tenderly brushed the snow off her back and they walked over to where he'd parked his motorcycle. Kelsey watched patiently as he secured his saxophone case in the rear rack with two bungee cords before climbing on herself.

"It's looking good. Did you get it detailed?" she asked, admiring his ride.

"Uh-huh, did it myself this afternoon." He smiled, handing over her helmet.

Brenden's bike was a vintage 1965 Hog, the one thing his dad had left him. It was his pride and joy — he kept it well oiled and in prime condition, the chrome polished to a reflective shine. Many people in town had offered him good money to take it off his hands but he always refused. Kelsey knew he would never trade that bike for anything. It was part of him, it made him who he was. Without the bike, he was just some poor kid in ripped jeans riding the yellow school bus. But with the bike he was Marlon Brando in *The Wild One,* Dennis Hopper in *Easy Rider,* an artist, a rebel, a hero.

He swung over to the front seat and rubbed his hands together for warmth as he shivered under his thin, tattered denim jacket. Kelsey felt a pang as she wrapped her arms around his waist.

She knew how much Brenden wished he could afford a proper leather motorcycle jacket, like the matte black one with the silver zippers they'd spied in the Harley-Davidson store in downtown Cleveland one afternoon. But the jacket cost more than four hundred dollars brand-new, and there was no way Brenden would ever have that kind of money. He worked part-time at a garage but all his paychecks went straight to the Stop & Shop to help his mom put food on the table. His father's alimony and child support checks never arrived on time, if at all.

But none of that mattered as Brenden kicked the Harley into gear and it revved up with a satisfying roar. As they drove off in the dusting snowfall, Kelsey pressed tightly against the strong back of the boy she loved, glad she was there to keep him warm.

School was out for winter break, so Kelsey dragged Brenden to the Parker Mall the next day, ostensibly because she had a coupon at Bed Bath & Beyond that she wanted to use to buy her mom a little something. Christmas was just a handful of days away. Sadly, with her meager allowance and the pittance she made babysitting, "a little something" was all she could afford for everyone on her Christmas list that year. But Kelsey was really at the mall to shop for *him* — she had saved up the most for Brenden's gift. Although she had no idea how she would be able to buy him a present that would show how much she loved him with only forty-five dollars — all she could scrape together and save on five dollars an hour.

Forty-five dollars! What could anyone buy for someone you loved with all your heart for only forty-five dollars? Kelsey wanted to buy him something truly wonderful, something that would show him how much he meant to her.

They walked past the roped-off Santa's House section, where crying kids were being escorted to sit on the bearded guy's lap. The mall was bursting with eager, last-minute shoppers who swarmed the stores, ignoring the Salvation Army bell-ringers and their red buckets. After a quick kiss goodbye, Brenden and Kelsey went their separate ways with the tacit knowledge that each was shopping for the other.

Kelsey walked desperately from store to store, feeling more and more discouraged at the dismal offerings her budget would allow. At the Sharper Image, she contemplated a battery-powered razor; at HMV, she found a *Family Guy* DVD that fit her budget; and at Banana Republic, wool sweaters were marked down to thirty bucks. But nothing seemed right. Too cheap, too generic, too lame — and certainly not worthy of someone as special as Brenden.

The lack of money in her pocket made Kelsey feel pensive, and not quite in the Christmas spirit. After a fruitless hour, she met up with Brenden at their designated meeting place in front of the Starbucks, and found he was similarly empty-handed.

"Get anything?" he asked.

She shook her head grimly. Her mood didn't brighten when they walked by the food court and she noticed a bunch of Wade Hill girls — minus Gigi — holding court at a primo table. Brenden immediately began to study the fast-food menu overhead with focused concentration.

"Hey," Kelsey greeted them, trying not to feel self-conscious in front of Gigi's circle. She couldn't help but wonder if they ever noticed that her jeans didn't have the tell-tale wavy line stitched on the back pockets like theirs did.

"Hiiii, Kelsey," they cooed. "Hey, Brenden." The group of popular girls all looked alike, from their shiny straightened hair and whitened teeth, to their cozy cashmere sweaters, and their matching football-playing, clean-cut boyfriends in their varsity letter jackets and faded Abercrombie button-downs.

"Where's Gigi?" Kelsey asked, glancing around.

"I think she's out with her mom, getting her dress fitted," a girl named Sarah answered excitedly. "Did you know? She's getting her hair and makeup done for the party by some guy from Chicago! He did J.Lo when she was on *Oprah*. Her parents are flying him in! She's so lucky!" Sarah sighed, her eyes wide with envy.

Gigi's upcoming Christmas Eve Party/Sweet Sixteen Bash at the sprawling McClusky mansion was all anyone ever wanted to talk about ever since the invitations — embossed on creamy card stock as thick as cardboard — had landed in their mailboxes. The party was to be the biggest event the town had ever seen. The McCluskys had even hired a catering company and booked a DJ from Cleveland. To Kelsey, it sounded nothing short of magical, like one of those parties where the celebrant arrived at the event in a Cinderella carriage or hidden among a group of undulating belly dancers like she'd seen on MTV.

"Ehmagad, it'll be so pimped out!" another girl enthused. "She told me they're tenting the backyard!"

"They've invited everyone in town," said a third.

"Well, everyone who matters!" a fourth corrected.

They all looked at Kelsey with anticipation. "You *are* coming, right?"

"I — I guess so, I mean, of course," she replied, looking at Brenden meaningfully. But her boyfriend was acting as if memorizing all the ingredients of a giant burrito was the most important thing in the world just then.

"Why don't you guys sit down?" a girl named Daphne asked, although her tone indicated she wasn't too enthusiastic about the prospect. Kelsey always noticed that the girls weren't as friendly to her when Gigi wasn't around.

"Yeah, sit down," Daphne's boyfriend agreed, a little too readily, and Kelsey noticed Daphne's mouth twitch in annoyance.

"Thanks, but we've still got a lot of shopping to do," Kelsey said, trying not to feel too insulted when she noticed the palpable relief on the girls' faces.

Brenden coughed and pulled on Kelsey's sleeve.

"Well, uh, good seeing you guys . . ." She smiled apologetically as they inched their way past the clique's brazen up-and-down stares.

✳   ✳   ✳

When they were out of earshot, and seated in a quiet corner with their food trays (a Diet Coke and a grilled cheese sandwich for her, a milk shake and gravy fries for him), Kelsey reached for Brenden's hands underneath the table. "Sorry about that, but if I didn't say hi they'd think I was rude."

Brenden released his hands from hers. "I just don't know why you care so much about what they think of you," he said.

Kelsey's father worked in a machine shop and her family was closer to the poorer side of things than the richer. They lived in a tidy little house off the main road with a front porch and a backyard that faced the woods. It was a decent neighborhood, a little run down maybe, a little more lower-middle class than middle-middle class. And Brenden lived next door. Their block was certainly nothing like Wade Hill, which was a mile away, up near the mountains, where large, stone, colonial-style manors boasted views of the lake and looked imperiously over the town.

Gigi's father was a successful oncologist at the Cleveland Clinic. It was rumored Gigi had enrolled at Parker only to have a greater chance at getting into Yale because of the geographical quota and the fact that she had no rivals for valedictorian. Her friends who'd prepped at Andover, Exeter, and St. Paul's would face stiff competition.

"They're just a bunch of dumb rich people," Brenden

complained, punctuating his sentence by pointing his straw in the air.

"You're wrong, I don't care what they think!" Kelsey protested, stealing a fry from his plate and dipping it in the pool of ketchup. "But I do want to be there for Gigi's birthday."

Gigi could be a bratty pain in the ass sometimes, but she was basically kindhearted. Their freshman year, she had even started a community outreach group to help the town's "less fortunate." Kelsey had joined the after-school club only to die of embarrassment when she found out Gigi had organized a charity food drive to help families in Kelsey's own neighborhood. Kelsey never explained to her parents why there was a basket of canned goods on their porch one afternoon. They ended up donating it to a homeless shelter.

To her credit, Gigi never brought it up, for which Kelsey was glad, and the two girls had forged a real friendship. Kelsey was the only one who knew Gigi's mom had battled alcoholism, and Gigi was always someone fun for Kelsey to gossip with. Most of the time, Gigi bit her tongue about Brenden, who certainly didn't fit into her version of what an "ideal" boyfriend for Kelsey would look like — i.e. preferably one who didn't have grease-stained fingers all the time. Gigi had even innocently inquired once why his parents had spelled his name incorrectly — the proper Irish way was "Brendan." Kelsey had briskly pointed out that their town was full of phonetically-spelled first names, like "Kitelynn" (Caitlin) and "Antwone" (Antoine) — not that it had helped her point much.

"The party will be fun, c'mon," Kelsey cajoled in the food court. "I really want to go."

She knew Brenden's reluctance to attend the party stemmed from an incident the past summer. They'd been invited to a Wade Hill picnic by the lake and Brenden had shown up in a pair of baggy denim cutoffs instead of surfer shorts like the rest of the guys. He was also the only one with two tattoos on his back — a leaping tiger and shamrock. But unlike the Wade Hill preppies, who were baby-soft and pink, regardless of their letterman jackets, Brenden was all tanned sinewy muscle, with a six-pack stomach and protruding hip bones.

"All right." Brenden sighed. "If you want to go, I'll take you."

"You're sure?" she asked keenly. "I don't want to make you do anything you don't want to."

"Do I have a choice?" he joked, raising an eyebrow.

"Not really," she admitted, feeling giddy.

"When have I ever said no to you?" he asked, blushing as she leaned over to kiss him smack on the lips in front of everyone in the food court.

"You won't regret it, I promise," she said. "Especially not when I'm wearing you-know-what."

Now that Brenden had agreed to be her date for the

evening — and her mind raced as she wondered how she could convince him to wear something more formal to the event — Kelsey finally allowed herself to be properly excited about Gigi's party. Because for once in her life, she actually had the perfect outfit to wear for the occasion.

In the far reaches of her closet hung a dress carefully concealed in a plastic garment bag, stuffed with tissues and worn only once before. A real Cristobal Balenciaga gown from the 1960s, made from the finest Parisian silk taffeta, given to her grandmother by the designer himself. A long, long time ago, Kelsey's grandmother had been a model in New York, and had even walked the runways of Paris and Milan.

Kelsey's mom still told stories about how her mother had been discovered by a visiting modeling scout at the bus station, and how she'd left the Midwest for a life of impossible glamour, dating wealthy men twice her age in the big city. Unfortunately, she had gotten pregnant by one of them — a married man, who promptly dumped her and disowned the child she carried. She returned heartbroken to Ohio and died shortly after giving birth to Kelsey's mom.

The year before, Kelsey and her mom were cleaning out the attic when Kelsey came across a dusty old trunk. Inside she found the remaining tokens from her grandmother's short life in the *beau monde* — yellowing magazine clippings of a slim, beautiful blonde whom Kelsey greatly resembled, Stork Club matchbooks, a PanAm plane ticket to St. Moritz that had never been used. In the bottom of the trunk was a gray plastic garment bag.

"What's this?" she'd asked her mother.

"Oh, I forgot all about it," her mom said wistfully. "It was my mother's and I've been meaning to give it to you one day. Open it."

Inside was a silver silk Balenciaga dress, cut with a dramatic scooped neckline, fitted through the waist, so small and fragile that at first Kelsey was worried it wouldn't fit — but it did, perfectly skimming her figure. The silk was as soft as rose petals. It was almost fifty years old, but the style was clean and classic, there was nothing dowdy or even faintly old-fashioned about it — it was modern, elegant, drop-dead gorgeous. It was her only real heirloom, the one reminder of a grandmother she had never even met.

The Balenciaga dress was the greatest treasure in her closet, and she'd been saving it for a very, very special occasion. She'd modeled it for Brenden in her room several times, but had restrained from pulling it out to wear to any of the school dances. Somehow, slow-dancing across the foul lines on the gym's basketball court just didn't seem to do the dress justice.

Gigi McClusky's swanky party, however, felt like the most opportune time to wear it. Everyone in town was breaking their bank accounts to be able to show up in their finest garments, and Kelsey was determined to look just as good.

They finished their meal and Kelsey, still feeling happy

about the combined prospect of finally wearing her dress and having Brenden agree to be her date, excused herself to go to the ladies' room.

She was just about to exit her stall when she heard the door open and the clicking of heels on the tile floor. Daphne's and Sarah's voices carried over the sound of the running water and hand-dryers, and Kelsey's ears burned when she realized the Wade Hill girls were talking about . . . her.

"Did you check out the coat? The fur is so fake!"

"She's not fooling anyone with that Kmart special."

Hello, it's from Old Navy, Kelsey thought indignantly.

"I can't WAIT to see what she wears on Saturday!" Sarah whooped, as if Christmas had come early.

"What are you talking about?" a new voice asked, and Kelsey recognized Gigi's level tones.

"Gi!" the girls screamed, as if they'd happened upon a celebrity. "What are you doing here?"

"My mom and I are picking out stuff for the gift bags," Gigi said. "I bumped into the crew at the food court and the guys said you were all in here, as usual. So what's up? What are we discussing?"

"What Kelsey Cooper's going to wear to your party," Sarah informed her.

"Probably that tired black sack she trotted out for Homecoming *and* Fall formals," Daphne snipped. "Don't you think?"

There was an expectant silence. The girls knew Gigi considered Kelsey a friend, and they wondered how she would react to such a nasty breach of etiquette.

Kelsey pressed her ear against the door, just as riveted to hear what her friend would say.

But the silence continued, and for a moment there was no sound but that of Gigi removing the cap from her lip gloss. "I guess," she replied, applying a wand to her practiced pout.

I guess. . . .

The words were like a blow . . . even Gigi thought she was a little pathetic for not having new clothes to wear. . . . Gigi hadn't even had the heart to defend her. . . .

Trapped in the stall, Kelsey's face burned crimson. *I'll show them. I'll show them all.* If they only knew what a prize she had hidden in her closet! The thought of her grandmother's Balenciaga dress was a balm on her wounded pride, but it couldn't take away the hurt she felt at Gigi's betrayal. How could she?

"I really hope she wears those pleather heels again, they're priceless. You know she actually told me they were 'vintage' designer?" Daphne chortled.

"Yeah, I hear that's what they're calling 'Payless' these days!"

"Oooh, snap!" Kelsey heard the sound of giggling and of palms slapping high-fives.

"Okay, cut it out!" Gigi chastised with a sigh. "Get your claws back in, why don't you? Give the girl a break."

Kelsey's hands were still shaking when she returned to the food court. It was just as she'd suspected — they all saw through her — saw through her discount clothes, the creative thrift-store outfits — they knew she wasn't one of them, and she never would be. They were privileged and pampered, not so much mean but spoiled rotten. They would never understand what it was like to not have everything they ever wanted.

"Hey, what's wrong?" Brenden asked when he saw the look on Kelsey's face.

"Nothing," she said, shaking her head, her eyes blinking rapidly. Damn if she would let those stuck-up bitches make her cry! *The dress, the dress — think about the dress. Think of how no one else at the party will be wearing a real haute couture gown.*

Brenden decided not to push it and they left the food court. Kelsey walked around in a daze until they reached the opposite side of the mall, and found themselves in front of Saks Fifth Avenue.

"Let's go in," she said, her eyes lighting up at the elegant display of sumptuous shearling coats and jewel-colored gowns on the mannequins. Saks Fifth was by far the nicest store in the mall, and although Kelsey knew she couldn't afford to buy anything they sold, she loved to browse anyway, getting a contact high from all the fabulous designer merchandise. Maybe it would make her feel better.

Brenden made a face but he followed her inside, slouching in his thin jacket.

Kelsey walked purposefully through the maze of glittering cosmetic counters, ignoring the black-clad salesgirls wielding perfume bottles like spray guns, straight to the shoe salon. *Payless indeed!* She browsed through the tempting array of magnificent Italian footwear, her heart beating quickly at the sight of such fashionable abundance. Luxurious crocodile pumps, sexy velvet stilettos, rhinestone-encrusted sandals with dizzying price tags . . .

And then she saw them.

Metallic silver leather strappy sandals, with a spindly wooden heel and skating-rink-size crystals in a vertical pattern from ankle to toe.

Oh, what shoes!

They were Choos, to be exact. The most exquisite pair of Jimmy Choo sandals she had ever seen.

"Look at these!" Kelsey cried, her hands trembling as she picked up the pair and showed them to Brenden.

"What's so great about those shoes?" Brenden asked, hands jammed into his pockets, looking out of place in his gas-station shirt and Levi's among the white leather couches. Brenden claimed that he never really understood her whole obsession with fashion, which he thought was kind of silly since Kelsey looked great in anything. He found fashion intimidating and elitist, a part of Kelsey's life and aspirations that excluded him.

"They're perfect," Kelsey breathed, stroking the sandals with reverence. "They'll match my grandmother's dress perfectly. The silver is the same *exact* shade." No one would ever laugh at her in those shoes — those shoes kicked serious ass — those shoes said, *I am stylish, hear me stomp!* They were a pair of man-killers, defiantly sexy, enviable to the extreme. With those Choos on her feet, the Wade Hill girls would surely shut up. Even Gigi would be impressed.

"Care to try them on, miss?" a salesman asked, appearing quietly by her side.

"I don't know," she said, shaking her head — try them on? Did she dare? She snuck a peek at the sole for the price tag — nine hundred and fifty dollars. Ouch! Was she even worthy of such decadence? But what could it hurt?

"You look about a six and a half?" the salesman purred. "I'll be right back."

"Okay," Kelsey said, feeling faint. She couldn't believe she was actually going to try them on — that they would be hers if only for a little while.

"Huh," Brenden said, gingerly taking a seat at the edge of the nearest chair and looking as if he would leap up as soon as anyone so much as looked at him the wrong way.

Kelsey sat down beside him, feeling like an impostor. Who was she to try on shoes of such craftsmanship and caliber? She couldn't even afford the tax on those things. Part of her was ready to flee, but before she could, the salesman returned bearing a lavender-colored shoebox, and knelt in front of her feet. He removed the lid and unwrapped the shoes from the crinkly tissue. The crystals refracted the light in a rainbow of brilliant colors.

Hypnotized, Kelsey removed her worn cowboy boots (bought for five bucks at the Value City thrift store) and peeled off her socks. She folded the hems of her jeans up to the knee and only then did she finally slide her feet onto the soles, wiggling her toes through the soft kidskin leather. She bent down to buckle the tiny little straps.

"What do you think?" she asked, looking up at Brenden, her eyes wide and shining. She straightened up and began walking, the high four-inch heels forcing her to walk with a seductive sway.

She smiled at Brenden — a dazzling, heartbreaking smile that lit up her entire face. There was nothing she wanted so much right then as the jeweled sandals on her feet, and yet at the same time she was fully resigned to the fact that they would never be hers to call her own.

Brenden studied her thoughtfully, and after a long time in which she thought he would never say anything, he clasped his hands tightly together. "I think you look absolutely gorgeous," he said at last. Then he broke his gaze and looked down at the carpet intently, as if the answer to the meaning of life could be found in its plush pile.

Kelsey examined herself in the mirror. What a star-studded entrance to Gigi's party she would make in her Balenciaga dress and these Jimmy Choo shoes! She could picture the jealous looks on her so-called friends' faces. Their jaws would drop right into their glasses of Red Bull and snuck-in vodka. But alas, she might as well have asked for the moon. The shoes were impossible to obtain — a glittering, adored prize that would forever be out of her reach.

"You think so?" she asked, shaking her head. "I'm not so sure."

"Miss?" the salesman queried. "Shall we wrap these up?"

"No, thank you," Kelsey said politely, sitting back on the chair. "They're not for me."

She unbuckled the straps with deliberate, reluctant grace, trying to keep her chin up, but all the while knowing that on Saturday night she would have to pair her grandmother's fabulous dress with her mother's old black pumps, which were too big for her and worn at the heel. Worse, those girls were right — they were made of pleather — "plastic leather."

"Ready?" she asked Brenden, when she could trust herself to speak.

*   *   *

A few days later Kelsey was beginning to seriously freak out about Brenden's present. The clock was ticking; tomorrow night was Christmas Eve. She caught a bus back to the mall by herself, determined to pick out something. Her budget hadn't changed — she still had no money of her own to speak of aside from the measly two twenties and a crumpled five. But she couldn't let Christmas come and go without giving him something.

She stood longingly in front of his favorite guitar store, twisting the ends of her sweater nervously, the shrill forced merriment of the piped-in carols making her antsy. She knew Christmas shopping wasn't about how much money you spent. It was about watching the face of someone you loved light up in happiness upon receiving a carefully picked-out present. Gifts didn't have to be expensive to be meaningful. But nevertheless she wished forty-five dollars bought something more substantial than a gift certificate at Radio Shack.

"Kelsey!"

She turned around. Gigi was bearing down on her, holding aloft her signature venti cup of soy-milk moccachino and a dozen overstuffed shopping bags from a variety of expensive boutiques.

"Oh, hi," Kelsey said, trying to muster the usual enthusiasm. She still hadn't quite forgiven her friend for what she'd overheard the other afternoon. Although technically, Gigi hadn't done anything wrong — she *had* asked the girls to quit it —

albeit *after* they had already raked Kelsey over the fashion coals. Gigi's lukewarm "I guess" wasn't exactly a stab in the back, but Kelsey felt like asking "Et tu, Brute?" just the same.

"You okay?" Gigi asked, smiling nervously, picking up on Kelsey's aloof manner.

Kelsey shrugged. "I can't seem to find anything for Brenden for Christmas," she admitted, although she would rather drink a gallon of her dad's gross eggnog before she ever confessed she was looking for a gift in the under-forty-five-dollar range.

"Totally! Boys are so hard to shop for," Gigi sympathized, smiling broadly. "I can't find anything for Jared either. I've been so bad! All I'm doing is buying stuff for myself. They have the cutest things at J. Crew — wanna go see? Maybe you'll find something for Brenden there."

Kelsey had no choice. She had to hang out with Gigi now, and give up the perfect-gift quest momentarily. Her friend dragged her from store to store, Abercrombie to BCBG, and with a sinking heart, Kelsey found herself inside the shoe salon at Saks Fifth Avenue once again.

Gigi tossed her bags on the ground and began barking orders to the scurrying salesmen, who hurried to keep up with her.

Kelsey walked over to the familiar display and found her beloved Jimmy Choo sandals on a Lucite pedestal. They were just as beautiful as she remembered.

"*Those* are cute!" Gigi said, suddenly appearing by her

side and scooping up the pair. "Can I get these in a six and a half?" she called to the nearest salesman. "For my party?" she asked Kelsey. "Don't you think?"

Kelsey's stomach dropped. Gigi probably wouldn't even wear them. She'd already told Kelsey how she'd picked out a sweet pair of the latest platform Gucci heels to wear with her dress when her family was in Chicago the other month. The thought of her precious Choos ending up in the bottom of Gigi's closet was almost too much for Kelsey to bear.

But the owl-faced salesman came back with a frown. "We're out of the six and a half, ma'am. I believe I sold the last pair this morning. I'm sorry."

Gigi grimaced. "Oh, well. I'll just take these Pradas then," she said, thrusting several pairs of shoe boxes at the guy.

Kelsey exhaled.

That evening, Brenden came over and they took a walk through the woods behind their houses to look over the ravine. The jagged edge of the sloping cliff opened up to a true wilderness. Growing up, they had chased each other through the forest of trees, falling over logs, collecting frogs, catching poison ivy. Every winter since Kelsey could remember they went sledding down the hill that ran by the frozen creek and afterward her mom would make them hot chocolate with puffy marshmallows on top.

"You've been quiet lately. What's up?" Brenden asked. He himself appeared jumpy and excited, on the verge of telling her something, but then he would bite his lip and look away.

Kelsey shook her head and inhaled deeply. The air was tinged with just a slight edge of burning firewood — a pleasant, smoky aroma that she always associated with Christmas. The moon shone above them, barely a crescent, before disappearing into the clouds.

"C'mon babe, talk to me," Brenden said, putting his arms around her and leaning his head on her shoulder. Usually it was Kelsey who tried to draw Brenden out of his shell, but not this time.

"I was just thinking . . ." She sighed. Thinking of Gigi's upcoming party, and all the anxieties that it had wrought — the dress, the shoes, the myriad disappointments before she had even stepped one foot inside the heated tents. Part of her wanted to be done with it.

Brenden rubbed his hands up and down the back of her coat, and she ran her fingers through his thick dark hair. He would be so handsome if he just wore it back, so that everyone could see his face — his sculpted, aquiline nose, and his deep, chameleon blue-green eyes. Eyes that were looking at her intently, as if trying to guess the secret behind her sorrowful mood.

They stood silently for a long time, just holding each other.

"Whatever it is that's bothering you, I'm sure everything's going to turn out all right," Brenden said gently. "It's Christmas after all."

"You're right, it's not important." She pressed against him, and they started with just baby kisses, a kiss on the forehead, the nose, the chin, and then she opened her mouth to his, and they kissed, with a growing passion, until his hands were no longer on top of her coat but underneath it, and up the back of her shirt. His palms rested flat against the small of her back, and she had dug her own hands underneath his denim jacket, inside his flannel shirt, and still they were kissing, and then he was kissing her neck, her clavicles, so softly that each kiss felt like a dance of butterflies against her skin.

Brenden buried his face in her neck and she hugged him tightly, suddenly noticing how much he was shaking from the cold underneath his thin denim jacket.

And that's when she knew.

She knew exactly what she was going to get him for Christmas, but more important, she knew exactly how she would be able to afford it.

Her hands suddenly felt clammy and cold, knowing the sacrifice she would soon have to make.

Christmas Eve morning shone clear and bright, and in her bedroom Kelsey was standing in front of her closet, contemplating a gray plastic garment bag.

Last night she'd made her decision.

The black leather motorcycle jacket. It was perfect — Brenden would look so kickass in it, riding on his Harley. It was tough, authentic, and well-made. Kelsey was sure he would love it as much as his bike. She'd seen the way he'd looked at it at the store when he'd come in to buy replacement grips for his handlebars. It would keep him warm, and it was just his style. She couldn't imagine him wearing anything else on the back of his bike. He would keep it forever, and would think about her every time he wore it, which would be every day, she was sure.

But the jacket cost four hundred dollars, when she only had forty-five.

Kelsey unzipped the garment bag slowly, taking out her grandmother's Balenciaga dress so she could see it shine in the light.

She caressed the whisper-soft fabric, the handmade label signed by the master himself. She was too practical a girl to regret never having worn it now. It was the only way. There were a bunch of vintage stores in downtown Cleveland, the city was famous for them — stylists from Hollywood and New York routinely made the rounds to cull the racks for the most fabulous vintage finds. She'd heard of vintage Pucci dresses selling for thousands of dollars, of Oscar starlets wearing 1950s Ossie Clark jersey dresses bought in Cleveland. What would they pay for a real, vintage Cristobal Balenciaga?

Well, she would just have to find out.

She quickly stowed the dress back in the bag, zipped it up, and walked out of her bedroom before she could change her mind. Downstairs, her mother was standing in the kitchen, making Christmas cookies with Kelsey's younger sister, Haley, who was eight.

"Hi, sweetheart. Want to help us make thumbprints?" her mother asked, her cheeks white with flour.

"Maybe later. Does Dad need the car?"

"No, he's sleeping. He worked late last night and he's off today, for once. It is Christmas Eve, after all."

"Cool, can I borrow it?" Kelsey asked, trembling slightly. If her mom said no, or if the car was out of gas or something, she wasn't sure if she could go through with it. She wasn't that brave.

"Sure, honey." Her mother nodded.

"I'll be out for a while, but I'll be back before dinner," Kelsey said, taking the keys from the basket by the door.

"Aren't you going to Gigi's party tonight?"

"Uh-huh," Kelsey called over her shoulder. "Brenden's taking me."

She drove quickly on newly plowed roads — there had been a snowstorm the night before, and the highway was slick and wet from salting. Her heart beat fast in her chest. There was an elegant vintage resale shop in the Coventry district, a neighborhood dotted with cool record stores, cute French bistros, and several resale shops. She'd been there several times before, and she knew the proprietress had an eye for designer dresses.

Kelsey parked the car by a snowbank and entered the cozy warmth of the shop, the garment bag draped over one shoulder.

"Hi," she said shyly to the stern-looking woman behind the glass counter. "Do you, uh, buy vintage clothes here?"

"Only if they are worthwhile," the owner said in a frosty voice. She looked at Kelsey, taking in the bargain coat, the jeans, the scuffed cowboy boots.

"Well, I have something of my grandmother's. I don't know, but I think it could be worth something." She laid the garment bag on the counter and unzipped it, removing the dress from its tissued environment. "It's a Balenciaga, from the fifties. It's only been worn once, I think. She got it in Paris."

The shopkeeper put on a pair of half-moon spectacles, and regarded the dress silently. Her wrinkled hands caressed the soft fabric. "My goodness."

"It's nice, isn't it?"

"How much do you want for it?" the owner asked sharply.

Kelsey was at a loss. She had never considered naming a price. She'd just thought it would be worth something — but what? She shrugged. "How much would you give me for it?"

"Three hundred."

Kelsey tried not to look too excited. Three hundred dollars! But then she remembered: The motorcycle jacket was four hundred. She noticed a few gowns hanging by the rack. One of them read HALSTON, 1975, $565.

"Six hundred," she countered, looking the woman in the eye.

"Four," the owner said.

"Five."

"Four-fifty, and that's my final offer."

Then the deal was done, and Kelsey walked out of the shop, clutching in her hand four one-hundred dollar bills, two twenties, and a ten. She'd done it.

She got into her car, shut the door, and blinked back tears. This was stupid, she thought. She'd *wanted* to sell it. She was doing it for Brenden. Her heart leaped when she thought of how he would smile when she saw his brand-new leather jacket! She drove straight to the Harley-Davidson store; she had to get there soon since it would probably close early for Christmas Eve.

A few hours later, inside her bedroom, Kelsey looked at herself in the mirror that hung over the door. The Wade Hill girls were certainly going to have a field day. She was wearing the same black dress she'd worn several times already. It was a simple, serviceable, average, black wool crepe with a square neckline, spaghetti straps. She'd purchased it on sale at the Gap for a fraction of its original price. She brushed her hair back until it shone, and carefully applied her makeup.

She took a step back from the mirror, assessing her reflection. She knew Brenden would be looking forward to seeing her in the silver Balenciaga. Would he be disappointed if he saw her in the same old dress? Would he still think she was the prettiest girl in the room? Next to the Wade Hill peacocks and all their new and expensive finery?

Kelsey clipped on her earrings — gold-tone hoops — and attempted a smile. So what if she was wearing the same old thing? There would be no grand entrance at the party, no star-making turn. She would just be one of the girls in the background. She chided herself for her girlish vanity; it was Gigi's birthday party, after all, not hers. Why had she been so obsessed with making a splash?

"Sweetheart, Brenden's here," her mother singsonged from downstairs.

She took a final pirouette, pulled up on the bustline to make sure it stayed in place, and then walked downstairs. The Coopers' living room had been richly decorated for Christmas — pine needles were scattered on the mantel, and the tree shone with multicolored lights, decorated with the handmade ornaments she and her sister had made in a succession of art classes — a wooden carved teddy bear with her name on it, Haley's handprint from kindergarten.

The fireplace was crackling, throwing off red sparks, and the house was warm and inviting. Brenden was waiting for her at the bottom of the staircase.

For a moment, Kelsey wasn't sure what she was seeing. "Bren — you're in a tie!" she exclaimed. "And your hair!" She almost tripped on the final step in her excitement.

She couldn't believe it. Brenden was wearing a proper sport coat and a dark tie. Gone were his dirty, grease-stained jeans and his ragged T-shirts. There wasn't a black armband in sight. He had even combed his long hair back, just like she'd always wanted him to, and she was right — without the hair in his eyes, he was even more incredibly handsome. Now everyone would notice, not just her. But why was he looking at her with that peculiar expression on his face?

"What's up?" he asked, holding a corsage in a plastic container and another package under his arm. "Where's your grandmother's dress?"

Kelsey pretended not to hear him. "I thought ties made you claustrophobic," she said flirtatiously, walking toward him, her fingers reaching out to brush his lapel.

"Yeah, well." He shrugged, trying to look nonchalant about his makeover. "But what's going on? Why aren't you wearing you-know-what?"

"Oh, that old thing." Kelsey tried to affect a careless laugh. "Forget about it. It's so old-fashioned, really, don't you think?" She kept talking, babbling, to cover up for her distress. He *was* disappointed. He kept looking at her with that strange, curious, blank expression on his face.

"What's wrong with this dress?" she asked a bit fiercely. "Don't you like how I look?"

"No — no. You look beautiful in whatever you wear, you know that, it's just . . ." Brenden shrugged his shoulders helplessly.

"Wait! I want to give you something. Hold on." Kelsey took the stairs two at a time and returned bearing a large white box with the Harley-Davidson symbol on it.

"Merry Christmas!" she said cheerfully. "C'mon, open it. Don't just stand there looking at it." She pulled him over to the couch and balanced the box carefully on his knees. Brenden put aside the corsage and his present for now.

He was speechless and stared at the box with trepidation, as if willing for the black-and-orange logo to transform into something else. Finally, he lifted the lid.

"It's the jacket you wanted!" Kelsey exclaimed. "See? Put it on! Let's see how it looks." She helped him take off his sport coat. "Now you can ride your Harley in style! And it's sooo warm. The guy at the shop said it's lined in sheepskin." Brenden nodded, putting on the motorcycle jacket.

"It looks fantastic!" Kelsey declared. She was right — he looked just like James Dean in it — or was it Marlon Brando? One of those old movie stars in those 1950s films that her mom sometimes watched. She bubbled over with happiness at how good her boyfriend looked in her gift. It was worth the sacrifice. Although she still couldn't get over how incredibly stunned he seemed — almost as if he were blindsided by her gift. Not quite the reaction she had expected.

"Don't you like it, Bren?" she asked, her voice quavering.

He finally spoke, and his features relaxed into his quick smile. "Of course I love it. It's from you," he said as he began to take off the jacket. He placed it gently on the couch next to him. "But here, I got this for you. So you could wear it to the party tonight." He handed her a silver box, wrapped in the signature Saks Fifth Avenue holiday paper — silver with red ribbon. "Merry Christmas, Kelsey."

"Oh, my God," Kelsey said, sinking back on the couch, not quite sure if she had the right to hope what she was hoping. "You *didn't*!"

Brenden smiled, leaning back on the couch and making himself comfortable.

"No way, no way!" she exclaimed as she ripped open the paper and opened the lid. But yes. There they were. She put her hands to her mouth, and tears sprang to her eyes, threatening to smudge her mascara. Brenden had bought them for her. The Choos. She felt dizzy with shock. How had he been able to afford them? The cherished metallic silver sandals — the crystal disks glowing in the box like diamonds. Gorgeous, and finally hers. The last pair in size six and a half. Her heart quickened to a frantic pulse. This was unbelievable, this was the best Christmas ever. Nothing had prepared her for this. . . .

"Oh, my god, Brenden. How . . . ?" she whispered, placing the lid back on the box and stroking it affectionately.

"Go on now, go change into that Balen-whatever dress and put 'em on," he urged, his eyes shining with delight. "Let's see how they look together."

Her grandmother's dress! The Balenciaga! In the excitement of the moment she had completely forgotten that it was no longer hers to wear with the Choos. Utterly miserable and devastated, Kelsey was afraid to meet her boyfriend's eye. In the smallest voice she could muster, she finally confessed. "I sold the dress to buy you the jacket."

"You . . ." Brenden said, trying not to look too alarmed.

"But don't worry, Bren — I can get it back, I can get on a payment plan with the boutique — once I have enough baby-sitting money . . ." Her voice trailed off hopelessly. The dress was gone forever — they both knew that.

He nodded slowly in comprehension, and rubbed his chin thoughtfully.

"But see, they look good with this dress, too!" Kelsey said, slipping off her mom's old heels and sliding into the precious Jimmy Choos. All right, so it didn't quite have the same effect as it would have had with the Balenciaga dress, but the shoes were still stunning.

She jumped off the couch and pulled him up. "I know it's

cold, but it's not a long ride up to the party. Do you have my helmet? Let's get on the Harley and go. I don't want to miss Gigi's grand entrance!" she added gaily. "Put on your new jacket now, c'mon!"

Brenden let her help him back into his new black leather jacket and they made their way to the front door. Kelsey flung it open and was flummoxed to find the street empty. Brenden usually parked his Harley right in front of his driveway next door.

"Where's the Hog?" she asked, looking around wildly. Slowly, she began to understand what he had done. *No.* She didn't deserve it. She didn't deserve him. . . .

"Babe," Brenden said, pulling her close and kissing her cheek, so she could feel his stubble. "I sold the bike to buy you the shoes."

He smiled at her, pushing a stray lock of hair back behind her ear. "We've got to take my mom's Dodge Shadow." He said, motioning to the rusty clunker hunkered on the street with the 1980s-style pastel brushmarks on the side.

Brenden, still wearing his tough biker jacket, wrenched open the passenger door to the decades-old compact car and Kelsey climbed inside.

Whatever would people say once they arrived at the party?

Then Kelsey realized with a laugh that she couldn't care

less what anyone thought — of her dress, her shoes, or her boyfriend. Especially what they thought of her boyfriend.

That Christmas, she had received a gift more precious than anything Jimmy Choo could ever offer or design. A gift that was truly priceless. She had received the gift of Brenden's heart. And even better yet, she had given her heart openly to him — and for that, she felt such an immense swell of happiness she felt as if her heart would burst from joy.

Brenden turned the key and winked at Kelsey as the engine sputtered to life. "What do you think?" he asked, reaching over to squeeze her hand. "We're a pair of crazy kids, huh?"

The Dodge Shadow inched its way forward in the snow, the tire chains scrunching on the gravelly road. It was freezing outside, and the car's heater hadn't worked since 1989, but neither of them were cold.

Hailey Abbott grew up in Southern California, and now lives in New York City, where she dreams about inventing the first combination surfboard/laptop. She is the author of the *New York Times* bestselling series Summer Boys.

"This story was inspired by my junior high boyfriend. He conspicuously disappeared from our friend's New Year's Eve party to kiss someone else. I was devastated, but his best friend (who was way nicer and cuter!) spent the night comforting me next to a bonfire he built on the beach. We officially became a couple at midnight, when he leaned over and kissed me!"

Melissa de la Cruz is the author of many books for teens and adults, including The Au Pairs and Blue Bloods series of novels as well as the forthcoming trilogy Angels on Sunset Boulevard. She has written for many teen publications including *CosmoGirl!*, *Teen Vogue*, and *Seventeen*. Her short story was inspired by the O. Henry classic, "The Gift of the Magi," in which "two foolish children most unwisely sacrificed for each other the greatest treasures of their house." It is a story she returns to every year during the holiday season, if only to

221

remind herself there is more to Christmas than expecting a mountain of silver boxes from Saks Fifth Avenue under the tree. She lives in Los Angeles with her husband, who has never disappointed her yet. Check out her website at *www.melissa-delacruz.com*

Aimee Friedman is the *New York Times* bestselling author of the novel *South Beach*, as well as its sequel, *French Kiss*, the romantic comedy, *A Novel Idea*, and the graphic novel *Breaking Up: A Fashion High Graphic Novel*. She was born and raised in New York City, where she still lives, and works as a book editor. Aimee got the idea for "Working in a Winter Wonderland" one magical Christmas Eve in the city, while walking along the sparkling streets and admiring the store displays. She wondered what it might be like to work in a glamorous shop for the holidays, and from that Maxine and her romantic misadventures were born.

Nina Malkin is the author of *6X: The Uncensored Confessions* and *6X: Loud, Fast, and Out of Control*. With "Scenes from a Cinematic New Year's," Nina wanted to tweak romantic tradition, plumb the redemptive power of love . . . and hopefully, scare you just a little.

Though a native New Yorker, she has never gone to Times Square on New Year's Eve, preferring to watch the ball drop from the comfort of her sofa, with her cute husband and two cats instead of a gazillion people for company.

DON'T MISS

Breaking Up

A fabulous and fashionable
new graphic novel
written by New York Times bestselling author
Aimee Friedman
and illustrated by Christine Norrie.

TURN THE PAGE FOR A SNEAK PREVIEW!